Daisy

The Autobiography of a Cat

BY

MIRANDA ELIOT SWAN

INTRODUCTION

This little story of one cat's life has been written during the intervals of a long and painful illness, when I missed the love and sympathy of my little four-footed friend of eighteen years, now, alas! nothing but a memory. Indeed, so vividly did his spirit speak to me, that I readily acknowledge him the author of this book, being myself his amanuensis.

From my earliest ch   ildhood the love of animals, particularly cats, has been inherent with me. One tale of cruelty, heard by me when a child, distressed me and made me ill, and nightly the panorama of the disgusting crime would haunt my pillow. But I never regret the suffering it caused me, for it taught me my duty to our dumb friends so dependent on us.

If the little stories in this book touch the hearts of its readers as that story touched mine, it will indeed have accomplished its mission. Just such stories are needed to create interest in the many societies now forming in aid of dumb animals.

There are cases where one must not spare the knife, even though our tenderest and most sensitive feelings recoil, for the cure will be sure. There are crimes perpetrated every day, in the name of Science, that need just such stories to expose their iniquity. For I believe ignorance is the cause of cruelty in many instances, and a little story told attractively, where retribution follows the deed, will have more effect than reproof. I do not believe there are many hearts so callous, that a little anecdote of cruelty to these helpless creatures will not touch them.

There are many who will read this book who have lost dear little pets, and I would say to them that the dear Father has them all in his care. In the boundless and beautiful fields of Paradise they will find the dear little friends they have lost waiting for them.

I trust my readers will pardon the many imperfections of this little book, believing that an earnest wish to help our dumb animals is my heart's desire.

MIRANDA ELIOT SWAN.

Boston,
December 11, 1899.

DAISY
THE AUTOBIOGRAPHY OF A CAT

DAISY
AN AUTOBIOGRAPHY

I
EARLY DAYS

I HAVE no doubt people will wonder that a Cat should write a story. Of course, fighting is more in their line.

However pleased I might have been to help my fellow-sufferers, and use my natural weapons in their defence, a remark I heard made by a very learned man decided me to use my brains instead of my claws.

He quoted:—

"The pen is mightier than the sword."

Taking this quotation for my text, I have written my own story, hoping it will benefit the poor cats who are made the victims of great cruelty. No other animal has to suffer like the household pet, the cat.

I am a Boston boy, born eighteen years ago, in one of the nice old-fashioned houses for which our quiet street was noted.

I was born in a clothes-basket, and do not feel ashamed of my birthplace, though fire and the swill man long ago removed all trace of it.

I cannot remember much about my home. Like all young things, my food and having a good frolic were all I thought of.

I loved my mother, for she was very kind to me while I depended on her for sustenance; but when I grew large enough to lap milk, she began to wean me and teach me that hard lesson—self-dependence.

My mother was very handsome—black as coal, with a long tail and white feet. She was very proud of the latter, keeping them as white as snow; and on account of their beauty she was called "White Foot." She was very graceful and slender—her fur soft and glossy as a raven's wing.

She had brilliant, restless eyes, fierce in expression and watchful, never seeming to trust even her friends. But every one was attracted to her.

We had not much room to boast of. The back yard was very small, but over the way a large unoccupied field gave us a grand opportunity to run and enjoy ourselves.

It was a great neighborhood for cats. Though I thought them rough and aggressive, I enjoyed myself, for I could outrun the biggest of them, and never allowed myself to be defeated.

One day my mother called me to her, and said: "I wish you to listen to what I am about to say to you. The cats who live here are rough alley cats, and have never learned good manners. You have a better chance than they have, and I hope you will grow up gentle and sweet-tempered. Never bite or scratch, and learn to control your angry passions. Then you will be a favorite and a very happy cat—happier than your mother, who never had a chance till now. And now it is too late. I shall not be with you long, and you must try to do the best you can for yourself when I am gone."

This conversation with my mother made me very sad, though I was young and full of frolic, and did not fully realize her true meaning. I never forgot her advice, for I knew she was a very wise cat, and her wisdom had been gained through suffering. My life with her was short, for she left us before I was six months old.

Perhaps here I had better tell her story as she related it to me. She had always been very strict with me, and taught me to be very neat, and keep my fur and my claws clean. My claws were a great delight to me, they were so sharp, and I used to bite them with great satisfaction. It was delightful to feel how sharp my teeth were.

Though I did not use a "toothpick," my nails were very useful instead, and I bit them and enjoyed the fun. But one day I bit them so loud that my mother, after reproving me many times, boxed my ears. She was very nervous, and the snapping provoked her very much.

Of course, I was obliged to obey her; but I bit them all the same, only on the sly.

II

2

MY MOTHER'S STORY

I DO not know where I was born. I can only remember a dark cellar where I seemed to belong, and children who drove and frightened me every time I went near the house. The cook was kind to me and put out scraps of food in an old tin plate. I was often obliged by hunger to pick from the swill barrel my dinners. I soon found plenty of rats, and after I learned to kill them, life had some charm for me.

It was a dirty, damp, dark cellar, for the people who owned the house were of the "newly rich" class. They thought only of decorating that part of the house open to public inspection. Everything was made to pay its way, and the servants were kept on short rations.

I earned my living (picked from the swill barrel) by killing rats, for the house was infested with them. No one ever spoke a kind word to me, and I often wondered why I was made. I would creep into the house like a criminal.

Once I enjoyed the luxury of sleeping in a chair. Oh, how soft and nice it was, and I began to purr, with the sense of happiness. But I was rudely shaken from my dream of bliss, and this was the only chance I ever had to test the delights of easy chairs. I was driven out with stones and bits of wood till I gladly found refuge for my poor bruised body in the cellar. There I lay in hunger and pain, my heart filled with bitterness toward all mankind. I felt the injustice, if only a poor cat.

It was a great neighborhood for cats, and I soon made friends with them. I was perfectly reckless, and caterwauled with them, joining their midnight revels with all my heart. We cared not for bottles or bootjacks, but made night terrible. Why should we keep quiet? We had no homes, no nice beds, no friend to speak to us. Why should we care to please those who remembered us only to abuse us?

Now this is all very sad. Since I have seen what life ought to be, in this dear home, I wish with all my heart I had earlier known these good people. I am very thankful that you, my only living child, will grow up in this refined atmosphere.

To return to my dismal history. Soon after my introduction to the nightly revels, I had my first kittens. I never was so happy in my life. Though I had suffered all alone the most severe pain, the dear little creatures compensated me for my hours of anguish. There were four of them. Two of them were black, and two of them gray. Such perfect little creatures, I was delighted with them. Though we had only an ash-heap for our bed, I kept them on my fur, and did not care for the ashes on my own nice fur coat. No mother on her bed of down, with laces and embroideries around her, could have kept her children nicer than I kept mine.

I followed just the instinct my Maker gave me, and what came after was from no fault of mine, but from the wickedness of human nature, which has unsettled my beliefs and made me a sceptical and unbelieving cat.

I hated to leave my kittens to take my food. How I fought for the best I could get, to nourish them! I swallowed things I had always disliked, for I was determined to carry back milk enough for all four of them.

This happiness lasted but a short time. The tyrant of the family, a dreadful boy of ten years, discovered them one morning. With shouts of delight, he took them and dropped them, one by one, into a pail of scalding hot water.

3

The cook called to him and tried to remove the pail, but it was too late; he continued his cruel work till my four dear little kittens were lost to me forever.

When I heard their last feeble wail, I tried to save them or share their fate. I was driven back with laughter, and the blows from a huge stick in the hands of the young murderer soon drove me down to the cellar, where I lay bruised, and oblivious of my pain and loss, for some hours.

Late at night I crawled out, faint and hungry, a hopeless outcast on the face of the earth. Tom, one of the neighbors' cats, shared his supper with me, and listened with sympathy to my sad story.

"Oh, is that all?" he said, when I had finished. "You may be glad they are dead, and out of the reach of that boy. If he is not hung," said Tom, with a wise shake of his head, "I miss my guess. Why, he is the terror of the neighborhood. He invents cruel things to practise on animals. Some time ago he cut a little baby pup's throat with a penknife, and sewed it up with cotton and a great big needle, while he never winced. The little pup died in great agony. And the boy's mother said, 'The dear child will certainly be a doctor, he has such skill.' Old Tabby, who lives next door, when she heard this speech of his mother's, said, 'He may be, and is, a devil, but he never ought to be a doctor.' And as we all believed in this wise saying, we gave old Tabby three cheers."

Tom tried to comfort me, telling such heartrending stories of the abuse of poor cats that my hair stood on end with horror. I then and there vowed hatred to all mankind. Even the peace of this dear home and the love of these dear people have not cured me of my distrust. I see an enemy on every hand.

Tom could not console me, and I was too wretched to confide my plans to him. I was suffering intense agony. My breasts were swollen like crab-apples. I could not bear the pain, and dragged myself to a puddle of water, hoping to cool the heat in them.

That night's suffering was the turning-point with me. I made up my mind I would take myself miles away from these cruel people, where every hand had been against me and mine.

I started slowly, and crawled through alleys and back yards, it seemed to me, for miles. The sound of a human voice, particularly that of a child, acted like a whip on me. I would run till my breath grew short, and I would sink down, feeling I must die, that I could never move again. Then at some sound I would start once more.

At last, worn out with fatigue, hunger, and fever (caused by my inflamed breasts), I reached a gate just as it opened to admit a man with groceries. I rushed in, spent and breathless, and hid myself in a dark corner. Here, thought I, will be a rest for one night.

As I crouched down in the dark corner, the man came out of the house, with the servant behind him, to close the gate. What an anxious moment for me! She returned to the house without seeing me, and I was safe.

After a brief rest, broken by the throbbing of my breast, I aroused myself, and, attracted by a bright light, I approached the window. The light came from the kitchen, where the half-curtain, open in the middle, gave me a glimpse of paradise.

This is the picture I looked upon with longing eyes: A large, old-fashioned kitchen, scrupulously clean, a table covered with a red cloth, a shade lamp standing in the centre, and a nice work-basket by its side, completed this homelike picture. The servant, a woman of middle age, nice, fresh, and pleasant looking, sat by the table, in a large rocking-chair, darning stockings. A more homelike scene never greeted the eye of a poor outcast. But the crowning object of all was a large black cat, spread out on a nice rug in front of the fire.

Presently she arose, walked about, swinging her tail, "monarch of all she surveyed," as I soon found she was.

How my heart beat as I thought, "Why is this? Why am I homeless, cast out to starve, while this cat has a beautiful home and is well fed and happy?"

Alas! even in the animal world is the vexed question, which disturbs human beings, of why one being, created by our "Heavenly Father," should be high in power, while others who are just as worthy are down under his feet. We ask, but who can answer?

Very soon, while I stood looking in, shivering with envy and my bodily pain, a door opened, and a lady came in. She was no longer young, but ladylike, and very kind and pleasant looking. She sat down and called, "Topsy, Topsy," in such a kind voice it made my heart ache. I looked with surprise, for Topsy took not the least notice of her. The lady laughed a very pleasant laugh, as she said, "What an odd creature you are," as she took Topsy in her arms, and smoothed her fur. Topsy did not seem to care for the affection lavished on her, never responding at all.

But just then another lady, somewhat younger than the other, came in. Topsy gave a great rush into her arms, and to my surprise, clasped her black paws around her neck, while the lady hugged and kissed her just like a child.

I could watch no longer. Envy, hatred, and malice, added to my swollen breasts, made me too wretched to live. I just dragged myself back to my dark corner and closed my eyes for a long time, oblivious of everything around me. At intervals I slept when the violent throbbing of my breasts would allow me; but when I could think, one idea had taken full possession of me, and that was a determination to get into this home.

"Surely," I said, "they have such kind hearts, they will not refuse help to such a miserable object as I am."

This comforted me a little; and as the neighborhood was a quiet one, and as I was worn out by the miles I had run and the pain of my bruises, I was able to sleep till morning.

The first thing I heard was a step approaching, and Bridget, the girl I had seen the night before, bent over me, saying, "Bless me! here's a strange cat in our yard." Then, as she looked again, she said in a sympathizing voice, "Poor creature! you look half starved."

She ran in, and soon returned with a saucer of milk. She held it to my lips, and I tried very hard to move myself up, that I might swallow. It was impossible; for the slightest movement gave me great pain, and I moaned and closed my eyes.

She then got an old blanket, and folding it nicely, she lifted me up tenderly and placed me on it. I tried to lap some of the milk, but the effort brought back all my pains. The anguish of my swollen breasts was more than I could bear, and I fell back on the blanket, hoping I should die. Everything was so peaceful that I had no desire to arouse myself to battle with life any longer.

"Here," I thought, "they will care for me and bury me, then I shall be with my dear little kittens perhaps."

I had no fear, but a great pleasure in a quiet death; for I knew that God would care for all the creatures He had made. I was glad to die and escape from persecution,—no more to be kicked and cuffed, no more be hunted by cruel children.

5

As I dozed off, I heard voices, and on opening my eyes I saw Miss Eleanor, the lady I had first seen the night before. As she bent over me, I thought her face was beautiful. Her eyes were filled with tears in pity of my suffering. She smoothed my fur with her soft hand, and when I moaned as she touched my breast, she exclaimed, "You poor creature! your breasts are like bricks. Look here, Milly," she called to her sister, "just see this poor cat's condition. What brutes she must have lived with, to treat her in this manner, taking away her kittens, and leaving her to suffer."

"Take her in, Bridget, and put her in Topsy's basket," said Miss Milly. "I wish I could deal with those people! They would never abuse another cat."

I was lifted tenderly and placed in a large basket, with a beautiful soft rug inside to lie on. Miss Eleanor bathed my breasts with warm milk, and then applied some healing lotion after the milk had dried. It kept them very busy, for the heat dried the milk as soon as it was applied. It was very soothing, and I tried to lick her hand. She was delighted, and kissed me right between my eyes, saying, "She is a grateful creature," while tears of sympathy shone in her eyes.

"This is heaven," I said to myself, "and I am perfectly happy here."

When Bridget brought me some warm milk, I was able to lap it very well.

"What shall you do with her?" asked Bridget.

The sisters looked at each other while Miss Eleanor said: "What will Harrie say? We cannot keep another cat with Topsy."

"We may find a good home for her, but it would be better to chloroform her than leave her to suffer," said Miss Milly.

The warm kitchen, the soothing cream, and the soft rug made me very comfortable, and I slept the rest of the day, trusting myself to these dear, kind people.

Miss Eleanor came quite often to see me, bringing me cream and soft bits of chicken, though, never having tasted such food before, I did not know what it was. I had very little desire for anything but water or milk, as the fever made me very thirsty.

Miss Milly came down later in the evening with the elder sister, the mistress of the house. Mrs. Rice was a sweet-faced little woman, and looked with great kindness on me.

"What shall we do with two cats? Topsy is a houseful. What will you do with her, Milly? She is so jealous if you touch another cat."

"I will manage her, for we must keep this poor creature till we find her a good home."

"You have a hard task, and when you introduce her to Topsy, 'may I be there to see.'" And Mrs. Rice turned away, laughing. "This bids fair to be the 'cats' house' that Eleanor used to tell the boys about."

"There is no use waiting," said Miss Milly. "If Topsy should find a cat in her basket, war would be declared at once."

This made me tremble a little, and subsequent events proved I had good reason for my fears.

Pretty soon we heard Miss Milly coming downstairs and telling my story to Topsy in a coaxing voice. She told it in so thrilling a manner that I never realized I was such a sufferer before. She came in, holding Topsy in her arms very tightly.

The moment Topsy's yellow eyes rested on me she gave a yell, and tried to escape, but her mistress held her fast while Miss Eleanor came over to me. I cowered down in the basket—not from fear, oh, no! Like the war-horse, I "scented the battle," and longed to measure claws with this proud creature. But I was wise. I knew I had a character to sustain and a home to earn. I kept my temper, closing my eyes as if too weak to open them.

"I think I had better take her in my arms, as this is Topsy's basket, and you know she never allows any one to touch it." And Miss Eleanor took me on a blanket, and held me on her lap.

"You are a naughty cat, and I am ashamed of you," Miss Milly said, as she put Topsy down.

She did not care for the reproof, for she glared and scoffed at me. Then she went to her basket, snuffing around it, till Bridget came, and taking out the rug, said, "Of course I must shake it, or Madam will not touch it."

She soon brought it back, and after a time Topsy seated herself bolt upright, and looked at me with such contempt, as if to say, "Never dare enter this basket again."

I never did, and never wanted to, as they found me a very good place in an old clothes-basket, and, to Bridget's delight, gave her a new one instead.

Then Miss Milly took me in her arms, in spite of Topsy's yells and frantic efforts to get at me, saying, "Now, Topsy, if I ever hear you have treated this poor creature badly, I will punish you, and love her best."

After this, though Topsy never cared for me, she treated me like a poor relation, offering me all the tough pieces of meat and bones; but she could never see me near Miss Milly without trouble.

We lived very happily in this nice house for one year. No one had cared for me, and I had settled down like one of the family, and soon my place was assured, for one day Topsy was missing. Everything was done to find her. Rewards were offered, and, for months, Miss Milly never gave her up, and it made her so ill that no one ever dared mention Topsy to her. I did pity them all, for they loved her dearly, but to Miss Milly it was like losing a child. She was always very kind to me, but she never was known to pet another cat till you were born. And I do think, Daisy, you can win her love, and in a measure console her for Topsy's loss.

It was a great mystery, her disappearance, for they never got one trace of her. One thing was very sure; she was stolen, for she never would have left of her own accord. Some one suggested that, being a "Salem" cat, she had gone home to the "witches," as all black cats are said to belong to them.

I missed her, but was very happy to be the only pet in the house. I had many kittens, and they were treated kindly, and mercifully disposed of. One was always kept till I could wean it, and then a good home was found for it. You were promised to a friend, but it was very fortunate for you that their delay in sending gave you such a hold upon the affections of these nice people that they decided not to give you away.

This pleased the boys, as they did not care to lose their dear little playmate. Miss Milly said, "Daisy shall be mine."

Great changes have come to this home. We have moved twice, and the good Bridget they could no longer afford to keep. We are now about to move again. I know they will provide for me, but I like this nice neighborhood, and the musicales on the back shed. The Bohemian blood in my veins I cannot ignore.

The trouble I have passed through makes excitement necessary, and I put my whole heart into the fierce fights, and enjoy them.

Why not? I know people say, "Cats! awful fighting creatures!" Well, but where are the bull-fights, in which man and beast shed each other's gore and men and women look on? Dressed in their laces and diamonds, they applaud while rivers of blood flow from the poor wounded victim. The genteel cock-fights, and hunting down one poor little fox by a pack of hounds! If we are cruel, we learn it of human beings.

I do wish I could be satisfied with a quiet life, but it is too late to reform, and I shall meet my fate here. I will not go with them. You, my dear child, will be the loved one to comfort them. And I charge you to profit by your mother's experience, and you will be a fortunate cat.

This is my mother's story as I heard it from her lips.

Two weeks after this conversation we moved to a small house, with only a few rooms. To me the change made no difference. I was happy, petted by all. It was no surprise to me that at the last moment my mother was missing. But it was a real sorrow to them all. They searched everywhere. They sent to all the neighbors, asking them to feed her, and let them know if she came back that they could send for her. How I wished I could speak, and tell them that one reason why she left them was the fear of being a burden to them.

For several weeks they never gave her up, but often went to the old place; but no one had seen my mother. At first food had disappeared that they had put out for her, but after a time it was not touched, and no one ever saw her again.

III
MY HOME

YEARS have passed since my mother left us. Though I never forget her, I am very happy with the dear people who were so kind to my poor mother, and I try to be a comfort to them.

No reverses of fortune have touched me. Mrs. Rice is very kind to me, though she is not so fond of cats as her sisters. The boys are just perfect. I love them dearly. Karl, the eldest, is a real tease. He pretends to his aunties that he does not care for me, but no one makes more of me (on the sly) than Master Karl. Will is such a dear little fellow! His love for me made them decide to keep me.

We had one long room, and the seam in the poor old carpet was very prominent. On this seam Will and I had our race-ground. He would run just on the seam, and at the end of the room would jump very high. I would run just behind him, and jump higher. This pleased them all, and we got many kisses and treats for our play. Then we would roll over and over, my claws and tail flying, and we did enjoy it.

I was usually very obedient, but sometimes I had contrary fits. It was the "Bohemian" blood in my veins that my poor mother so often spoke of. I cannot get rid of it, and it makes me do something naughty. One cold day, just before Christmas, when I was nearly five years old, I ran away. The door of the laundry was open, and without a thought I rushed out. No one missed me. They supposed I was in the laundry. I mounted to my seat on the fence, and just turned around to find a comfortable place, when a strong hand seized me from the other side, and I was carried swiftly down the alley and taken into a strange house.

I was received with open arms. Not one word of reproof was given the big boy who had stolen me, for the wickedness of the act. They asked him, "How did you manage?"

"Oh," he said, "I was looking over the fence, to see if the stuck-up Rices were there, when I espied my Prince, and grabbed him."

"What shall we do with him?" asked the boy's mother.

"Shut him up till he forgets his old home."

(How little they knew about a cat's nature, when they thought I could forget!)

I rushed into a corner, and struck out with open claws at all who approached me, growling just as I had heard dogs growl—an accomplishment I had just discovered. Delighted with my success, I was inclined to make the most of it.

"Well, I must say he has a nice temper." And the bad boy held up his hands, where my etchings, though painful to him, were a credit to my skill. "King Karl and Prince Will must be covered with scars. Who cares! If they won't play with me, I have got their pet cat, and will keep him, in spite of his beastly temper."

"No, you won't," I said to myself, "if I can help it."

For three wretched days I was shut up. They treated me with great kindness, and tried to pet me, offering me nice food. I was too homesick to care for anything, and too wretched to think of eating, only that I had sense enough to know I must take enough to give me strength. I could not sleep. Visions of my dear home and loved ones kept my eyes wide open, and I did make good resolutions never to run away again if I could get free.

The big boy went away to spend the holidays, leaving orders with them all to keep me, that when he came home he might enjoy the sorrow of the Rices.

"They have sent around slips to all the houses and have advertised, but they shall never get him," he said, with a horrid laugh.

After he had gone, finding I was no pleasure to them, they decided to let me go. They could tell the boy, when he returned, that I ran away. They were not people who regarded truth at all.

So one day I found the door open, and without waiting to say good-by, I ran home. I had been away three days. It was the day after Christmas, and it seemed to me three years since I left my home.

Stacy Knight, a dear little fellow about Will's age, the son of the friends in whose house we had rooms, happened to be in the basement, and espied me when I jumped on the window. He gave a real Indian yell as I rushed into his arms, and we mounted the stairs, two at a time, and found ourselves in the midst of the family assembled in the hall, wondering at the war-whoop given by Stacy.

My dear mistress sat down on the floor, hugging me in her arms, while all of them were ready to take me from her.

"Oh, Daisy," she said, "what a sad Christmas we spent without our pet! Where were you?"

I could not speak and tell her what it had been to me, and they never knew where I had been. After this I always looked on both sides of the fence before I seated myself.

After they had all caressed me and expressed their delight at my return, dear Mrs. Knight said:—

"Now that 'The Prodigal Son' has returned, he must have a party."

"Yes," said Karl and Will, "we had no Christmas; let's give Daisy a tree."

After Stacy, Karl, and Will had indulged in a war-dance, and each had turned me heels over head, they all decided it would be a nice plan. And from that time till the New Year's night, when the party was to be given, we could think of nothing else.

IV

DAISY'S PARTY

GREAT preparation was made for my party. I was truly a fortunate cat. I could not help them work, but rushed to and fro from one to the other, knocking down spools of cotton and everything I could get at, jumping up in their arms, disarranging their work, and trying in every way to amuse myself; but when I was wanted to try on my clothes, I would rush under the bed and elude even the longest arm. Then Will would crawl under the bed, and, after a good frolic, would land me where I was needed.

Mrs. Rice made a tall black hat with a cockade on it. She had to tie it on with strings, for as soon as she put it on I jerked it just as I had seen monkeys do.

Miss Eleanor made me a pair of red pants, leaving a good slit for my tail, for I was to represent a monkey, and the tail was very important, though, as my mistress said, no monkey ever had such a beautiful tail as mine.

Miss Milly made me a dress-coat, with white ruffles at the neck and wrists, brass buttons, and a white shirt front.

They covered a large pasteboard box with green cloth, for the organ. Will and his friend Josie were to be the organ-players.

The long-looked-for day came at last. I had raved up stairs and down, as Miss Milly said, "just like a maniac." I superintended all the preparations, walked over the tree that they were to decorate in my honor, and scratched it well, as they said, sharpening my claws for the evening. I was too busy to take a cat-nap or one of my "forty winks."

We had before this eventful day rehearsed our parts, and I had provoked them with my stupidity. I did make fun enough with that hat. I hitched it on the back of my head, getting out first one ear, then the other; for they had tucked my ears in, saying my face looked so innocent without them. It was all mischief, for I intended to do my best.

Mrs. Knight threw open her nice rooms, and in the hall room off the back parlor the tree was placed.

They were obliged in the afternoon to keep me prisoner upstairs. I was disgusted, for I wanted to be in the thick of it all. I could not sleep, and I kept pretty near the door, ready to run out if I could get a chance.

At seven o'clock they dressed me in all my finery, and before eight all our guests had arrived: Madam A., a lovely woman, and one of our best friends, with her three noble boys, and a sweet-faced little bit of a woman whom every one who knew her called cousin; then Madam M., with her daughter and granddaughter,—charming people, and all my dear friends. These, with Mr. and Mrs. Knight and their son Stacy, with ourselves, made a party of (reckoning myself) seventeen,—quite a roomful.

I thought (and I can assure you a cat's opinion is of some value) that the Queen might be proud to see such beautiful, refined, and highly educated people at her drawing-room. To be sure, there were no décolleté toilets, but then it was a proof of the good sense of the people. Of course the Queen would not admit cats to her receptions; it would not be safe. The bones would be a temptation, and I fear cats would not respect even elderly bones, or spare them though decked with diamonds. I am happy to say that my party was purely democratic; they were really all my equals.

The back parlor door was thrown open, and we were in full view of them all. The three boys in ragged clothes, bare legs, old shoes, were as hard a looking crew as ever accompanied a hand-organ. Will had the organ strapped to his back, and I sat upright on it. I was tied to Will's arm, and Josie held another string, for they could not trust me, fearing I would run under the sofa, at the expense of my tall hat and my dignity.

We were greeted with a burst of applause. The boys so successfully assumed the street gamin air, and looked so thoroughly demoralized, as they pulled their forelocks in recognition of the greeting, that no wonder they brought down the house, and for a short time obscured my august self. Stacy and Will gave a song in nasal style, pretending all the while to grind the organ, while I was mounted on Will's shoulder, swelling with importance.

Then they began "Yankee Doodle." Josie shook the castanets, Stacy beat the drum, Will ground the organ and sang, while they all danced like street Arabs.

I was perfectly beside myself. Oh, if I had only been Balaam's ass, wouldn't I have made a speech! I ran to and fro on the organ, then rolled over and over, my hat on one ear, my coat up my back, around my neck, and my tail wagging from the red pants, in fine style.

The boys looked on in wonder, for it is needless to say that this act was not on the programme, but an impromptu act of my own—and it was the crown of the performance.

There were a few songs after this, but nothing like our "national air." We could rest our laurels on that. I was handed around, kissed, and admired to my heart's content. My clothes were pronounced perfect; and then, when the boys went upstairs to change their clothes, my mistress removed my finery, much against my will, and I made it very hard for her by sticking my claws into the clothes as she tried to take them off.

Chester and Henry A., with Karl, were the ushers, and they opened the door of the hall room, where the tree was displayed in all its beauties. Mrs. Rice made a little speech, while Miss Milly held me tight, for, regardless of etiquette, I was eager to rush for the tree.

As soon as she released me I made one jump on the table, and discovered what my sense of smell had led me to expect,—three little fishes tied with a red ribbon. I soon had them off the tree and on the floor, and made inroads into them before I could be prevented.

Karl read the labels on the articles, while Chester and Henry distributed them, for I was pleased to see that my dear friends had been remembered as well as myself.

Miss Milly had a book of "Familiar Quotations." On the fly-leaf was written in Madam A.'s lovely handwriting:—

"To my dear mistress, whose motto has always been, 'Love me, love my cat.' Mew translated, 'God bless her.'—Daisy.

"Hang sorrow! Care will kill a cat; therefore, let's be merry."

I was very much pleased that the gift, purporting to be given by me, had just the nice selections I should have made.

The tree did look lovely. Karl had lighted all the tapers, and it was one blaze of light. There were very pretty paper decorations of bright paper. Mrs. Rice said, sometimes taste was better than money. We had little of that, but we had such warm friends we were very happy.

I had a pack of cards a little over an inch in length. They were a great pleasure to us. Will would spread them on the floor, and I would roll over, scattering them about. Sometimes he called me a knave, sometimes a king or queen, but I did not care, only for a good frolic. I had a box of pennies for my meat, a paper of catmint that I enjoyed, and a nice kidney done up in pink paper, some white, soft candy I loved, and last of all Miss Eleanor and Miss Milly gave me a lovely collar and padlock. I was proud as a prince with it on my neck.

There were nice little gifts for all my dear friends; but the best of all was, that on them were written nice little texts and—"From Daisy," just as if I had given them myself. It proved that they understood how well I loved my dear ones, and how gladly I would have given if I could. It was better than all my own gifts, though I enjoyed them very much; but this understanding of me, making me one with them, made me feel like a cat-angel—and then and there I became a Christian cat.

Then we had ice-cream and cake handed around by the boys. I had some in my own little pewter plate. Miss Milly melted it a little, but I had very small appetite for it. I was so excited that I could not keep still enough to lap ice-cream. I had licked the kidney, tasted the fish, chewed a little catmint and was quite hilarious over it, as it always went to my head. My tail had more to do with it than was agreeable to the company; for I whisked it about, greatly to their disgust: they did not like being dusted with catmint. Miss Milly said, "I shall be obliged to give you a dose of nux vomica, for I fear you have eaten too much of a mixture for even a cat's stomach to digest." I just winked at her, finished licking my ice-cream, then I kicked over the plate, making it roll under the piano. This provoked a shout of approval from the boys.

Then we had a little music. Chester and Henry A—— played nicely, and my one dear girl friend also played, but she preferred playing with me. I was very fond of her and always responded to her affection.

Then my nice party broke up. No one of those who were there will ever forget it, I know.

Ah me, how long ago it seems! The boys and my one girl friend are twelve years older, while I am an old cat. Mamie, my friend, is a graduate of the Boston University. She will make her mark some day. The boys are Harvard graduates, while our own boys are Brimmer and High School boys.

They can all talk in many languages which I, of course, can understand. Some of them will be smart business men. Chester, I think, will fill a professor's chair, while the others will represent the law. They will all achieve greatness if the love of one cherished cat can make them.

I know there is a warm corner in their hearts for Daisy. And however hard the world has used them, they will read my little book and keep green in their hearts the memory of one who loved them dearly, when she is sleeping peacefully under her namesakes, the daisies.

Perhaps they will tell their children about their cat friend, and read to them this little story of one happy cat, who was made a member of the family and a friend of all the nice people who visited them. It will teach them kindness to their little four-footed playmates, and they will realize that warm hearts beat under their little fur coats.

V
REVERSES

I PASS over several years—very sad ones to us all. The breaking up of our home, the death of dear Mrs. Rice, I cannot write of, though Time, the true friend of the sorrowful, has laid a healing balm on our hearts. Miss Eleanor and Miss Milly were both prostrated by their sorrows, and we were obliged to go into the country for a change of air.

How carelessly I looked upon the preparation for our flitting! When I mounted the piano, my favorite seat for many years, I little thought it was for the last time—that I should never hear my kind friends play on that dear old piano again, that I should never again arouse them in the morning by walking over the keys when they had left it open at night.

I could not understand their tears, when the furniture and piano were carried away, that they were parting forever with things associated with their old home and those who had made their happiness, now gone forever. Yet when I saw only our trunks, and looked at their sad faces, I did wish I could be something better than a cat and be able to help them.

I tried to amuse them, acting over all the little tricks they had taught me, and was a very happy creature when Miss Milly smoothed my fur, saying, "Oh, Daisy, what should we do without you!" Then I realized I was a comfort to them.

They had bought me a large brown straw basket with a cover, and very strong handles, and when I walked into it, taking possession, I felt like a prince of the blood. I little thought how many miles I should travel in that basket! It was open in places to give me air, and I could lie down and turn around comfortably in it. When travelling, my mistress would keep her finger between the cover and the basket, and with my eyes fixed on her face I felt safe. She said she felt under a spell, to watch me, and my stony stare reminded her of the Stranger Guest, in the "Ancient Mariner."

We remained only one month in our first boarding-place, for it was not satisfactory. The cats I could not associate with, for they were rough tramps, no one owning them, and they had no care. I was very sorry for them, knowing how care and kindness could transform them.

They really hated me, and it made me very unhappy, my chief offence being my collar and padlock. They might have overlooked my collar, but the padlock was adding insult to injury. Their eyes would grow green with envy that one of their race should be above them. They looked upon my collar and padlock just as women look at each other's diamonds. Animals feel envy the same as human beings; only they can tear and rend each other, while their so-called superiors would like to do the same were it not for the power of the law.

Cats and dogs fight, and that is the end of it; but with human beings it is never forgotten, and makes them bad-tempered and tyrannical.

I was very sorry for these poor cats, though I could not understand such mean feelings. I was always pleased when I saw cats or dogs with pretty collars on and bows of ribbon. One lovely white cat I knew used to wear blue ribbons, and I always told her how nice she looked, till I found how vain she was; then I said no more about her good looks, for I do hate vain people. I would gladly have given my collar and padlock, though I loved it dearly, if it would have helped them.

It is a problem beyond one poor cat's solution to know just how to help people to understand our race; but I do hope this little story will help a little. The life of one petted cat perhaps may make others as happy as I have been.

We changed our rooms quite often on our return to Boston; many of them were so cheerless I will not speak of them. Whatever our discomforts were, I was always cared for; but I did wish I could provide a palace and servants for my dear friends. I remember the stories Miss Eleanor used to tell the boys, and I wished I could be Cinderella, with a fairy godmother to give me means to help others. I fear I should have killed the mice before they were changed into horses. And when the boys would say to their aunties, "Why don't you have horses and carriages?" I also asked the same question.

I am an old cat now, and I know, and do not ask such questions, for I understand the world better, that it is not to those who deserve the most that luxuries are given. Why, we will never know.

We lived in one house where we were very uncomfortable. Our room, to be sure, always looked bright and nice, but it was because we had such good taste in covering up our defects and making poor things look nice.

The lady who owned the house was a philanthropist. It is a long name for me to master, but I thought it over in my waking hours, just as my mistress pronounced it, and I can think it quite correctly, better than I can understand why she was so called. She was utterly neglectful of the two gentlewomen in her house, who were far ahead of her in education and culture, if not her equals in money.

I pondered the name, and its meaning, more and more. I will not say it made me tired, for that is slang; but it did make me sleepy, and I would drop into a good cat-nap right in the midst of defining "philanthropist."

She had a cat named "Oliver Twist." One must have some companionship of his own kind. So Miss Milly said, "Perhaps he will be a playmate for Daisy."

"Perhaps," Miss Eleanor said, "he also may be a philanthropist."

We soon found, however, he was nothing of the kind. He proved himself a most depraved cat. Under the cloak of virtue he concealed a very coarse nature. He never came up to our room without trying to provoke a fight. His black, beady eyes and sleek Maltese coat always irritated me. I had a cattish desire to fight him and let him know his place. For my mistress's sake I tried to subdue this feeling, remembering he was my guest, and I must be polite even at the expense of comfort.

It was all thrown away on him; it was "casting pearls before swine." When I went out into the yard, as I did every day for an outing, he would hunt me about, as if I had no right to be there. Not one scrap of food did I ever get down there, though he was always ready to have a feast when he came to us.

One day things reached a climax. I had tried to amuse him; he had taken my favorite chair, and washed himself all over in it, leaving so many hairs on it I thought I should go wild, knowing how Miss Milly would have to clean it. I gave him half my milk, and though he stood with one leg in the saucer to keep me from eating any, I still kept my temper. I would not make a fuss. But when, after finishing my milk and licking his chops right in my face, he flew at me and knocked me down, then I threw all politeness to the dogs, and unsheathing my claws, I closed with him, rolling over and over till he yelled well. Like all bullies, he was a coward.

My mistress said, "Daisy, I am ashamed of you." Miss Eleanor took "Oliver Twist," and put him out, with scant ceremony, saying, "I wonder what Charles Dickens would say to hear a cat like that called 'Oliver Twist.'"

"Poor cat! You know he is disciplined by a philanthropist." And Miss Milly laughed at the absurd thought.

I laughed also, as I crept into a corner, when I thought how nicely I had "Oliver Twisted" him. I slept the sleep of the victorious. I did not see very much of him after this, for we went early into the country for the summer.

There were very nice people where we boarded. One dear little boy was very fond of me. He hugged me so hard I avoided him. My mistress told his mother that she did not think children should be allowed cats and dogs for playthings. Miss Eleanor talked quite nicely to little Alec, and I think when he remembers her stories of children who were good to animals, that it will make him careful, for he was a nice little fellow, and he may be a good friend to poor ill-treated dogs and cats.

I enjoyed that summer very much. The cats were kind and friendly, and the beautiful trees on the grounds gave me a nice chance to run up and hide from my mistress. She was anxious about me all the time, fearing to lose sight of me. She used to pet all the cats that were good to me, and they all said, if they had a friend like her, how good and happy they would be. Some of them were very wild and rude, hunted as they had been by bad children, and scat from the door when, half starved and cold, they had sought shelter and friends. No wonder they were not nice company for well-bred cats. I did pity them and never turned away when they came near me.

At the end of the grounds was a big bed of catmint. It was like the "corner grocery store" for the cats. Crowds of them would assemble there to talk over their affairs. And when, excited by the power of the catmint, they would get into a row, though there were no pistols or murders, such as characterize human fights, there were black eyes, scratched faces, and hate and rage in plenty.

I kept out of it all, though I cannot deny that my heart beat faster. I had to sheathe my claws till they hurt me; but I thought of my position, for a well-brought-up cat can understand the meaning of "noblesse oblige." I suppose I felt just as men do (and women too, as to that) when they bet on the fighting parties. And I had my favorites as well as they, and knew who I hoped would win.

I did love that catmint bed, and never for one moment doubt that in the boundless green fields of Paradise we shall have acres of catmint where we can roll to our hearts' content. I did try to encourage the poor neglected ones with this prospect, but they did not believe me. They said I was a "cat fanatic," "a fool," "a revivalist." They said, "If we are to be so cared for, then why don't your 'heavenly father' that you think so much of do something for us now?" And they all talked at once and were so excited, they hissed and yelled so loud, that my nerves were all of a quiver; but I stood my ground, though they pressed on me very hard, and breathed so much catmint over me I was glad when my mistress, hearing the row, came and took me away.

It was many days before I visited that catmint bed again, for it rained very hard. Miss Eleanor remarked that Daisy was rather quiet; she feared he was sick. I could have told her my heart was sick, trying to solve the problem, how I could reform my race, how make people believe them the intelligent beings they are.

After this I had to bear jeers and scoffs; but I would not give up my principles nor yet my catmint bed. Many were the scratches Miss Eleanor got, pulling me out from under the bushes, for the smell magnetized me. She always got me by the tail or leg, she cared not which, so that she carried me home and saved Miss Milly anxiety.

The people were very nice to me. One quiet young man, an artist, was very fond of me, and said I would make a fine subject for a picture. I used to flourish my tail and hold my head on one side just like a fool, I suppose; but then I know I am a beauty. I hear it every day, and how can I help being vain?

Before returning to Boston we paid a short visit to one of our friends. She had a delightful home, and the children were very much pleased to have me visit them.

As I have quite an adventure to relate, where I did not distinguish myself, I will take another chapter, and give it in full, without extenuating my faults, leaving them to be judged by my readers.

VI

15

DAISY'S ADVENTURE

THE eldest son and daughter were very kind to me, and I thought them just lovely. Their mother was an old friend of mine, and always when she came to Boston I was delighted to see her. I would jump up in her lap—a favor that I did not often grant to any one. Cats can tell who are true and who are false. I could have given my mistress points on this subject, for she believed in those she loved, and was often deceived.

There was a dog and cat that were great favorites with all the family. Spot, the dog, was very plain,—a great lanky creature,—but he had one virtue; that was obedience. Tom, the cat, was a hard-looking creature, but they all loved him dearly.

Of course both dog and cat hated me. They thought I put on airs, and they resented the affection their mistress gave to me. I walked about the garden, regardless of their hisses and growls; and they very soon got tired of it, when they saw I did not notice them. Mr. George, the eldest son, had Spot in complete subjection, and Tom dared not approach me when the family were near.

Miss Eleanor and Miss Milly were invited to the seashore. They had decided not to accept the invitation, as they could not take me with them. Mrs. H. urged their going, saying: "It is just what you both need,—change of air. I can take care of Daisy; it will be a pleasure." So it was decided.

When they kissed me at parting, and said, "How can we leave you, Daisy?" my heart ached so that I was too wretched to live. Had not Mrs. H. held me tight, I would have followed the carriage that took them away from me. Spot and Tom looked anxiously on. They thought, "Is this upstart to be left here to rule over us?"

Mrs. H. said that Spot must be kept at the store, only coming home at night. She tried her best to have Tom friendly with me, but a more obstinate cat I never met. He would stay in the room with me, and once took his dinner out of the same plate after they had kept him hungry a long time; but never could they make him friendly with me. I tried to be just to him, knowing how hard it was to have a "handsome, fashionable" cat, as they called me, come into their home and share their friends.

And then there was that collar and padlock. How much I suffered for that little bit of finery! And yet I loved it dearly. I never struck an attitude (as my mistress called it) without my padlock was in full sight, just under my chin, where I had placed it.

How long that one week was to me, and I am ashamed to say how many disgraceful acts I was guilty of. One night the climax was reached, and then my character was ruined for that family. I slept in the room with Mrs. H.—much to her husband's disgust.

It was a nice lounge I had, with a blanket on it, and any cat might have been happy there. Tom was envious of it, for one day he walked in and was just about to jump up there for a nap, when I jumped up before him, and gave a powerful hiss right in his face. He was all ready to fight when his mistress came in and giving him a shake, said, "If I ever hear you hiss at Daisy again, I will punish you."

Poor Tom! He knew he was unjustly accused, but what could he do, and I did feel mean, but what could I do either? I could not speak. I might have hissed; then, she would have known who was the offender. I did not, however, but just glared at Tom when she carried him off.

One night I could not sleep. I was homesick. So I just walked over the bureau, clinking the glasses and toilet bottles, and then mounted the mantle, meandering about sure-footed, though I did kick over a wooden ball, for pure mischief. I threw it on the floor, where it crashed down loud.

16

Mrs. H. started up, saying, "That cat is on the mantle; she will break the vases and clock."

"Let her break them," Mr. H. replied; "we shall get off cheap if that is all the mischief she does." And he went off to sleep again.

When Mrs. H. reached the mantle, no cat was to be found.

"Oh, Daisy," she said, "there you are, so demure, sitting on that chair! You are just like your mistress, so cute, no wonder she loves you dearly."

After coaxing me to lie down on the lounge, she went to bed, and soon fell asleep. I could not sleep, however. I had a restless desire to go and find my friends.

The end window was open at the top; it faced on a narrow piazza that extended the length of the house. It was gravelled on the top. I was very agile, and giving one spring from the top of a chair, I soon reached the window, and overlooked the situation. A good jump, and I landed on my feet, and walked along, crunching the gravel as I went.

I passed the bath-room window and then approached the window of Mr. George's room, which was open wide, but protected by a heavy screen. Here I planted my paws and looked in. One wild yell and a succession of barks rent the air, and Spot, who had been sleeping at the foot of his master's bed, rushed for the window and would soon have dashed through the screen and finished me,—for he was a powerful dog,—but his master's hand on his collar restrained him, with the other hand he reached for his pistol, thinking there were burglars about. His mother's voice at the door arrested him, and he opened the door, to meet her anxious question, "Is Daisy safe?"

"She is safe enough," he said; "but are we safe with a cat like this one in the house?"

"Take Spot into my room," said his mother, "while I get Daisy." In spite of her alarm, as she approached the window, she could not help laughing. "Oh, you cunning creature!" she said; "just as composed as possible, looking from one to the other, as if to say,—'Why, what is all this fuss about?'"

Sure enough, I stood with my paws on the window-sill, and did not move till she came, and removing the screen took me into the room where all the family were assembled, in undress, while Spot's loud barking could be heard from the next room. I was taken into the guest chamber, where Mrs. H. remained with me; for she said she was convinced no one could govern me but my mistress.

Two days more, and I was made happy by the sight of my loved ones. Mrs. H. did not tell them for a long time of my naughtiness. They said their visit was pleasant, but without me they had decided never to go away again. They said their friend had given them an invitation for me when they visited her another year. And it was really true. The next year they did take me; and as it is all fresh in my memory now, I will jump one year and tell you all about it.

I saw the cats they had told me about. One was called "Forepaugh," and she did look just like a real circus cat. She had one brown and one blue eye. The other cat was called "Spring." I liked them both very much. They were not educated cats, but they had good manners, and were very kind hearted.

Forepaugh told me sad stories of the cats around. She said very few people made them members of the family, as we were. Most of the cats were tramps, living in the fields and woods, afraid of every human being, having to steal or starve. They were naturally antagonistic to cats that had homes. They never had known kindness and could not believe in it. She said if ever a missionary was needed, she thought it was right here.

She said that just below, near the poorhouse, was a large field called "Cat Swamp," because all the cats for miles around congregated here. Some "dudes" had altered the name to "Feline Meadow."

"Cat Swamp" held the fort, however, as the most appropriate name. Here the cats yelled and caterwauled and told all their trials and sorrows caused by mankind.

The fights were fearful, and the heaps of fur to be seen around after one of these encounters proved in reality that there was nothing ideal in the tongues and sounds heard in this region. They said there was no help for it; people could not be made to realize that cats had a claim on them.

For several nights I had noticed one of the neighbors' cats sitting on the fence and listening intently to our conversation. This evening she came nearer, and gave a groan, while Forepaugh was speaking to me of the neglected cats. At last she said if she might be allowed to express an opinion, she had one all ready. We said at once how glad we would be to hear her.

"Suppose," she said, "some of your good Boston people, with their little tracts on the treatment of dumb animals, come along! What then! We can't eat their tracts, or live on them, can we?"

I didn't like to answer this cat, she was so big and aggressive, and looked at me with such spite, as if she thought I liked tracts, and the people who carry them about, when I do despise them. Finding I did not answer, she continued:—

"There it all ends. A lot of women will get together, with a few men thrown in, and they will talk and talk, going all around Robin Hood's barn, till they lose the thread of their discourse, and we wish some big bat would rush out and catch the thread and bring them to the point. Then they argue and draw up resolutions, and call upon the brethren to agree to them, which the poor men do, because they are afraid of the sisters' tongues. Then they are exhausted, and are obliged, 'as weaker vessels,' to drink gallons of tea, and the men smoke acres of cigars, and it all ends in smoke and tea grounds for us poor cats. The women think about each other's clothes, while the men are wondering if the women are rich enough to support them, should they propose marriage. Naturally cats are forgotten.

"Sometimes they find a home for a good-looking cat, but it is not a satisfactory one. Such people are not supposed to know much about people with hearts large enough to take interest in cats. They are handed over to high-toned servants, to pet and snub in alternation. The poor no-tailed horses, made wretched by the abominable check-rein and the flies, hate everything that moves, and kick at us. The liveried servants smoke in our faces, swear, and spit on us, till we hide ourselves in disgust and wonder if animals have dirtier habits than human beings.

"When the family returns to the city the house is closed, and these Christian people leave poor Pussy behind to look out for herself. Is it any wonder that cats have no faith in any one? That they join the midnight revels, and fight, and steal, to keep them alive?"

She was very sarcastic, but Forepaugh said it was all true; that cats were cast off just as if they had no right to live; then when they steal some bit of food, they are given a bad character and hunted about. They are expected to have better morals than human beings.

Forepaugh said that she had a real respect for this cat, that she knew all the cats for miles around, and helped them all she could; she said that hearing their tales of sorrow had made her cynical.

"I had thought her disagreeable," Forepaugh said, "till one night I saw her tugging along the remains of a big fish which a neighbor who had been out fishing had given her. I had the curiosity to follow her. She had to take a rest frequently, for the fish was heavy. At last, after walking a long distance, she dragged it over a stone wall. Soon feeble voices greeted her, and two half-starved cats that had been abused by bad boys raised themselves up, while their friend tore the fish to pieces with her sharp teeth. I got over the wall and helped her. They all were shy of me and inclined to sneer because I had a home, but I said I did not care; it made me mad, but I put all my madness into tearing up the fish, and they satisfied their hunger."

Forepaugh also said that their friend, not satisfied with feeding them, began to lick one of the great wounds made by a sharp stone thrown by a boy just for fun. Then, as they were thirsty, they dragged themselves down to a brook at the end of the field, and after drinking they were very comfortable. Then they told their trials, and said, "What can we do to make people kind to us?"

Forepaugh said she had heard of a Dr. Angell, who was devoting his life to helping dumb animals. They all yelled and scoffed when she said "Angell," saying, "Do you believe there is an angel in heaven that would look at a cat?"

Forepaugh said (being a Christian cat) she was shocked. She explained to them that it was the name, though she said, "I am sure it is appropriate, for he has proved himself one by his help to all helpless creatures."

"Well," they said, "we wish he could see us and help us. Why can't some one speak to him? Perhaps, though, he will think cats beneath his notice."

Forepaugh said she had often thought she wished she could see him and tell him about their sufferings. She said, "I always respected that cat after that night when we walked home by moonlight, after taking care of those cats; and when she sat down on a stone, saying, 'I must rest, for I feel faint; I have had no food for some hours, for I knew that fish would be only enough for them,' I said, 'You shall have some of my supper,' and I got her some pieces of meat and gave her all my milk, and went to bed happy, though I was rather empty."

After this I did have a real friendship for Forepaugh, and I told her if ever I could, I would try to interest this good man in our race. I had not then thought I should ever write a book, but now is my chance, and somehow I do feel he will help us.

The cynical cat never would make friends with me, but I did admire her, and I feel how small my life is compared with hers. Here am I, petted and living in plenty, and I can only be grateful and try to be a comfort to my dear friend.

Forepaugh told us that at one of the great shore houses they had a cat called Prometheus.

"Oh," said our cynic, "how I wish we could get at his liver; we should never want for food."

I pondered over that speech, and one day I heard my mistress telling her little niece, who was reading mythology, the story of Prometheus, "who was bound to a rock, vultures feeding upon his ever growing liver." It was very funny for a country bred cat to be versed in mythology. I suppose, however, she heard it, as I often do things my mistress and her friend talk about, and the liver made her remember it.

I was heartily glad to return to Boston, and I made up my mind I would let cats and all the animals I could reach know that they had not met the true philanthropists, but the shams that take up every new cause and dishonor it. For there are many earnest, true philanthropists who spend money and publish nice tracts in behalf of animals, and thus, in a measure, the tracts "do feed" animals; for they open the eyes of those who perhaps have never thought of the matter earnestly.

I determined, after my visit to Beverly, to write this book to help my unfortunate race.

VII
CAT MEMORIES

OUR new room, a very large alcove, was pleasant and comfortable. The people who owned the house were school-teachers, refined, and the atmosphere was congenial to us all. I loved to watch my friend's busy fingers and follow Miss Milly's pen, as she wrote for hours at her desk. I loved to walk over the fresh writing and flirt my tail over the ink-bottle. That would make her stop and scold me, then pet me till I was willing she should return to her work. The eyes of affection are sharp. I saw with pain that they were obliged often to lie down, after a long spell of work, but they never complained.

Mrs. Knight came often to see us, but I did not see Stacy for a long time. He was busy with his studies at Harvard, but he sent me kind messages, and I knew he loved me. Our boys were not with us, and I had no young company; but then, I was happy for I could see and hear from our young friends frequently.

I always greeted dear Mrs. Knight with delight. She had a camel's hair shawl she used to roll me in, when we lived in her house, and I loved to claw it and pull the wool out of it. I wondered she did not wear it, but then, I suppose, it was old fashioned. She told me that her cat Solomon was very fond of it, and she allowed him to sleep on the lounge with that shawl under him.

I felt a little jealous of Solomon, but I doubt if they ever love another cat as well as they love me. They said Solomon had no associates, though they lived on the swell avenue.

The cats belonging there were only tolerated one-half the year. The cats that were not boarded out were left to become tramps. Of course these cats were very immoral, and they did not think it would improve Solomon to be friendly with them. I did smile when Mrs. Knight said, "Daisy is such a perfect cat, we hold him up as a model for Solomon."

I wondered how Sol would like that, for he told me he did not like being kept in. He guessed he could take care of his morals; the society cats could not hurt him.

One day he proved himself not so wise as his name would indicate. He fell out of the third story window. When they gathered around him, thinking he would have to be chloroformed, he got up, shook himself, and lived.

He told me very sad tales of the cats living in that vicinity. "Would you not think," he said, "that in these palatial houses there would be room for one cat?"

I said I should think they would want two or three. He shook his wise head, saying, "Oh, no. If they see a cat that pleases them, some superannuated spinster will gush over her, making her a pet for a little while. But let poor Pussy fall ill, or get one flea on her, and out she goes into outer darkness."

"Oh," I said, "don't speak like that! my two dear friends are 'maiden ladies,' and no one can be kinder to animals than they are. The sick and unfortunate always appeal to their sympathy, and not in vain. I remember Miss Eleanor washing every day a poor neglected black cat whose eye a rat had bitten. It was not a pleasant piece of work, I can tell you, and she tended that eye so faithfully that it got well. They would go hungry to give food to a poor animal that needed it."

"Well, well, it may be so," said Sol, impressed by my indignant protest; "but I have heard that old bachelors and old maids are always the hardest on animals."

I indignantly denied this. "It is married people who dislike each other and cannot get free, who have horrid children—they are the hard ones. They do not want the care of their children themselves, and expect animals to offer themselves to be tortured by these wretched children. And if they defend themselves, refusing to have their eyes poked out with sticks, tin pails tied to their tails, and lighted matches held to their noses, and bite or scratch, then they are denounced as vile, and are given bad characters that will follow them through life."

I had spoken with real feeling, and I could see that Sol believed me.

"You are right, I suppose," he said. "We are both of us fortunate cats; 'our lives have fallen in pleasant places.'"

Poor Sol! He was so wise he had to quote Scripture, even if he did not understand it; and in this he was no worse than human beings. Do half of them know the meaning of the passages of Scripture they quote so confidently?

"We," he continued in a sentimental tone, "cannot realize how hard it is to be outcasts. These closed-up houses and boarded-up doors are gloomy enough during the summer months. At dusk the skeleton forms that steal out, too feeble to mew, start at every sound, fearing the stones and jeers they are sure to meet from the stray ragamuffin children who roam about this deserted region. Their hearts are broken,—for cats have hearts, and loving ones too,—and it is hard for them to believe that those who have sometimes noticed them have left them alone. I do not know," he continued, "where we are going, but I do not believe we were made in vain, and I think these heartless people will find in the hereafter that the animals they have abused will be avenged."

"All I desire," said I, "is to be with my two dear friends." And to this Solomon said, "Amen."

I like Sol very much. He is a very well educated cat and looks upon life in a serious manner. He has grown quite large and appreciates his good home. I think he is a Christian Endeavorer, and will do all he can for homeless cats. I remember his wise words; and when dear Mrs. Knight brings me some of his catmint, I enjoy it for itself, because I love it, and in memory of his friendship. One can remember his friends even if he does not meet them often. Perhaps if we were to see each other every day, we should disagree.

VIII

AN ACCIDENT

WE had a very nice home in the country offered us, which we were very glad to take advantage of. The people who owned the place, going to the seashore, preferred to have their house occupied rather than shut up, doing no one any good.

It was very pleasant there, and we had a very delightful time, though the accident which nearly cost me my life, and from which I shall never recover, happened there.

It was the day before the Fourth of July. Miss Milly had been to Boston to the funeral of our beloved Doctor. Miss Eleanor being too unwell to go, we kept each other company, and sad enough we were.

When Miss Milly returned, she was thoroughly worn out with grief at the loss of her dear friend and Doctor. It was a great loss to me, for I had been his special pet. During our dear Mrs. Rice's sickness I watched for his daily visit and knew his ring always. He would say: "Well, Daisy, how is your health to-day? Put out your tongue." Which, with Miss Milly's help, I would do. Then he would take my paw and feel my pulse in the most sober manner.

How nice it was! I would not give up this memory for a great deal of money. I could tell by his face just how our dear invalid was, and when he told them his skill was in vain, and that he could not save her, I saw the tears in his eyes as he took me in his arms. He was a perfect gentleman, and we all loved him and respected his great knowledge and skill.

We were sitting on the piazza talking about him, when I saw something move over under the trees. Supposing it might be a squirrel, I went to interview him, thinking that if I could kill something I should feel better. My mistresses were so preoccupied that when they went in to tea they never noticed that I had not followed them.

Finding no squirrel, I sat down under a pine tree, thinking about the beautiful flowers and the music Miss Milly had told us about, at the church funeral of our friend, and mourning that I should never see our dear Doctor again, and wondering what Miss Milly would do without him, when a rush, and a bark, and before I could face around a fierce bulldog buried his teeth in my shoulder. I fought for my life, though I felt the odds were against me. But let him kill me; I would die game. I did claw his eyes, blinding him and giving me chance to escape.

I crawled over the grass, then through the fence, into the neighboring estate, and hid myself in the bushes and deep grass. Then I lost consciousness. At times I realized my pain, and my brain was clear, for all my past life passed before me.

How beautiful seemed my dear home and friends, that I should never see again! Then the old childish days, when I had frolicked with my poor mother, came to me so vividly I could smell the sweet clover where we played; and then the dreadful pain and faintness made me realize the end was near.

I said, "I shall see our dear Doctor, and he will say, 'Why, Daisy! Have you followed me so soon?'" It was all dreamy; another fainting spell had come on, and it was nearly morning before I was again conscious. Then I thought, "I must try to see my dear mistresses once more, even if to die in sight of their windows." I was half crazed when I thought of their sorrow.

With the greatest effort I raised myself up, and it was nearly an hour before I reached the tree, the scene of yesterday's disaster. Inch by inch I crawled along, with all the courage I could command. If cats have nine lives, I lost eight of mine on that journey. I could not see; my eyes were closed up by cobwebs, from the bushes I had crawled under when I hid myself. I felt my way along, and when the tree was reached fell down exhausted.

Soon I heard a soft step, and Miss Eleanor gathered me up in her arms, trembling with fear that she should hurt me. She cried out with pain when she saw my bloody side, with the skin and fur hanging down nearly a quarter of a yard. She folded her apron, and held me in that, as I could be moved easily in that way; and I never winced, though the least jar hurt me, closing my eyes, and feeling I could die in peace. She carried me upstairs to Miss Milly's bedside.

Poor Miss Milly! She had not closed her eyes till toward morning, when she fell into a doze. She opened her eyes when Miss Eleanor spoke, and screamed with pleasure when she caught sight of me. She held out her arms; but Miss Eleanor said, "Do not move him." Then, when she opened her apron, and Miss Milly saw my torn and bloody side, she cried as if her heart would break, saying, "He will die! What shall we do?"

"Dress yourself quickly, and we will see what can be done. One comfort: he will be with us, and will have our care, even if we must lose him."

They folded a blanket, laid it on a wide lounge, then covered it with a clean sheet folded thick, and laid me on it. Then Miss Milly soaked off the cobwebs from my eyes with warm water and a soft cloth, and I could just see a little; but it was like a view of heaven to see their dear faces once more.

I tried to lap some warm milk, for the fever had made me thirsty. The effort was too much, and I fell back, faint and dizzy. When this attack passed off, I took a few drops of water from a spoon, and Miss Milly sat for an hour patiently, giving me drop by drop, till my parched tongue and throat were relieved.

She sponged around the wound, soaking the clotted blood from my fur so tenderly that I suffered very little.

My heart was so full of thankfulness that I would not murmur at my pains. And I do not think it was such a great virtue, though the suffering was fearful, for I think animals bear pain always with more fortitude than human beings.

Miss Eleanor went into Boston as soon as possible. Mrs. Knight was very much distressed, and at once went with her to see the great doctor for animals, Dr. Watts. He said he could not leave his office the Fourth of July. He said he thought my shoulder bone was bent, and as I was so old, he should advise bathing, without trying to have it operated upon. He gave them a liniment, saying he did not think I would ever get over it.

Miss Milly said he evidently thought me an old cat, and that I had better die than live and suffer. "He shall not die," she added, "if we can save him."

The liniment was just fearful, Miss Milly held my head in her arms, covering my eyes and nose; for it was very strong, and drew tears from their eyes. Miss Eleanor applied it slowly. I winced and moaned, but tried hard to restrain myself, for I knew they were suffering with me. And I was anxious to bear it; for somehow I had faith in Dr. Watts, and I believed it would help me.

Never had a patient better care. They made me catmint tea, and rubbed it on their hands so I could smell of it, and never left me alone. They kept the sheet smooth under me, for I could not turn over. It was like heaven to me, and after I had slept a little while, I opened my eyes, and seeing Miss Milly bending over me, I purred and put out my tongue to lick her hand. She kissed me with delight, and both of them caressed me, saying, "He will live, and no matter how much trouble he is, we will be only too glad to do for him."

It was very true. From that day I got better slowly. I could turn over, and the hanging skin and fur fell off; and they kept soft greasy handkerchiefs on the wound till it closed over and healed. In two weeks the fur began to grow, and soon I had as lovely a coat as before my accident.

Just one week did I keep good, because I could not help myself. Then, one day, they went down to dinner, leaving me asleep on the lounge.

I said to myself when I awoke, "This has lasted long enough; I will not be an invalid longer." I crawled down and surprised them. They gathered me up, and carried me back, saying: "You will not get well so soon if you behave like this. We will close the door when we leave the room after this, for we see that you are not to be trusted."

It did put me back, but my one desire was to get about, and I was soon able to. My shoulder was stiff, and it was a good six weeks before I could walk about with comfort. I limped a little, but my mistress laughed over it, saying it was an aristocratic limp—like some old gentleman leaning on his gold-headed cane.

It was due to the love and care of these dear friends that my life was saved—another debt added to the long list of favors I received from them. I hope my little book will be successful and prove how much I loved and appreciated them.

23

I have never been strong since my accident. There were internal injuries, and I often have an inward fever and great pain. I keep it to myself when I can, for if they find my breath feverish and my paws hot, they are very anxious and dose me with aconite and sometimes oil. Aconite I can take, but I do just hate oil. I act like a bad boy when it is given to me.

My misfortune had one bright side; it gave us nice neighbors. Very congenial ones they were.

When my mistress left me, to go in to tea that afternoon, they thought I had followed them, and had not missed me. Two tramp children shouted at the window, "Missus, your cat's killed! We seed a dog kill him."

They ran out to question the children, but could get no satisfaction. Then they called, "Daisy, Daisy!" all around the house and grounds; for they could not believe I was lost. The children must be mistaken.

There were some young people playing tennis on the Anchorage grounds,—the Admiral's place opposite,—and they came over when they saw Miss Eleanor and Miss Milly, and said they had seen the attack. They said the loud barking of a dog and a scream from the girl who was wheeling a baby carriage called their attention. They thought Daisy was killed; they saw him move, but could not tell in what direction; they said they did not believe it could be far off, as he must have received his death wound. The dog was a fierce bulldog, and belonged to the girl who had screamed. She had wheeled the carriage off quickly and called the dog, who was howling and bleeding from the encounter. They said, had they only been able to get a pistol, they would have shot the dog at once; but no one dare interfere with an enraged bull dog. And they had no time, for it all passed so quickly.

They came over and very kindly helped in the search, going down cellar, looking in the cold air box, and over the grounds. Where I could have taken myself so quickly, they could not understand. After their dinner they searched again—without success, however.

The Admiral's charming daughter, with her friend from a neighboring place, was very kind, calling the next day, trying to comfort my distracted friends.

It was after twelve o'clock before they went into the house; then they could not rest, walking out on the piazza, or sitting in the bay-window, and starting at every sound or shadow. Miss Milly said if they could only give me Christian burial, she could bear it better. It was a night never to be forgotten by them, and they loved me more, if possible, for what they had suffered when they thought they had lost me.

The young ladies I was soon quite intimate with. They brought ice-cream and jelly to me, and beautiful flowers. Of course we understood it was a delicate attention offered through me; in fact, it was using me as a "cat's paw." We had nice times sitting in the porch or on the piazza. They were so bright and chatty, talking about books they had read. I could not read books, but I could sit on them and look wise, and I never was known to scratch one.

In the next house were two pet cats. One was Maltese, the other black, with white breast and paws. They were very large and dignified. There was one singular feature about them: both had double thumbs. After I became acquainted with them I asked them why they did not join a circus or museum. Oh, my! how mad they were, for they were very proud and exclusive; and at first were very shy of associating with me till they saw what nice company we had. They said they thought we must be poor, for we kept no servant.

I told them we were poor, but we did not judge people by their money; that I guessed that so far as brains and culture and good breeding were concerned, my mistresses could beat the neighborhood, if we did not keep help. Then I pushed open the screen door and banged it in their faces. I was so very mad I never looked at them for a long time, and kept on the piazza at the other side of the house.

I did forgive them, however, but it was after their pride had a fall. The family, went away for some weeks, and the house was closed. They left the small door in the barn open, and a heap of straw, with a blanket over it, for them to sleep on. They engaged the man who cared for the places around to provide them with milk and food; and he was very faithful to them.

How we did pity them! I held up my head and walked away when I saw them, and Miss Eleanor said she did not think I could be so hard-hearted; but I could not stand it when I heard a piteous mew and saw a sad face looking at me, and I at once threw all resentment to the winds and went out with them.

After this they were in our house all the time. As soon as it was light, over they would come, and wait till we came down to breakfast. They went home reluctantly at night, and Miss Eleanor was so good to them she went with them and poked up the straw and shut them in for the night. Miss Milly would say to her: "Did you tell them a bear story? And did they say their prayers?" Miss Eleanor would laugh, and say: "I did pity the poor lonely things; they looked like the babes in the wood when I covered the old blanket over them. Only I thought they had a good, nice auntie instead of a wicked uncle." For, as you will see, I had been told all these stories, or the boys had, and I listened to them.

These cats were very nice to me. They would run up the trees and on top of the bay-window to amuse me; for I could not run or climb very well, though the next year, when we were out there, I could run with them very easily. We had such nice dinners together; for I enjoyed sharing my good things with them, and they were very nice about eating. They did not snort and growl as some cats do, or pick for the best. My mistress used to put down one large platter, and would give each of them the end, while I had the middle. Each shared alike.

We had a great deal of company. I enjoyed them all, particularly the artists. I had an eye for color, though I could not make a telescope of my paw and put it over my eye, exclaiming: "What perspective! What color! What technique!" But I could open both eyes and see if the pictures were true to nature.

Many offers were made by the artists to paint my picture; but my mistress refused them, saying: "Should I lose my Daisy, I could not bear to see a picture of her. I should always carry one in my heart, and would need no other."

Our pleasant home we left the last of September, just when the autumn foliage was in a blaze of color, giving us a delightful picture to remember through the winter. We carried home some pine-cones for our grate, and bright leaves to put in our vases—a very pleasant reminder of our summer home.

We made a pine pillow. I say we because I pulled out the pine as fast as they picked it. At last they were obliged to put me in the closet. I climbed on the shelf and knocked down boxes till, in self-defence, they released me.

But the pine pillow was finished, and I had many good naps on it, remembering those with whom I had played under the pines.

IX

25

CAT TALES

I HAD always felt desirous of hearing the history of Topsy. My mother lived one year in the house with her, on good, if not friendly, terms. Her disappearance was a subject I pondered over quite often. Naturally, having taken her place in Miss Milly's affections, I wondered about her.

One day my curiosity was gratified. A friend, very fond of cats, who had known Topsy very well, called. Miss Milly told her this interesting story.

Topsy was a Salem cat, and no one could doubt her being a real witch cat. She was nervous, always on the jump, and "such a smart temper!" Miss Milly said: "I had always been very fond of black cats, but it so happened, though we had cats of all colors, we had never a black one, till the arrival of Topsy. You know," she laughed, "I have always been very proud of calling myself a Salem witch. I have a mole on my left shoulder, and now that the black cat had arrived, I felt that I had all the requirements needful to make a veritable 'Salem witch.' I believe there is some superstition about a black cow, also; but one could not go about leading a black cow quite as well as a cat, and I felt satisfied that would entitle me to the name."

This is the way Topsy came to my mistress: One summer evening a friend drove up to the door with a basket of flowers. Miss Milly was pleased with them, but when under the flowers a little fluffy ball revealed itself, and when the little ball had brilliant yellow eyes, she was delighted. She smoothed its soft fur, saying: "What a lovely kitten! Is it for me?"

As she asked the question, the kitten gave one spring and landed on her shoulder, where she secured her position by sticking her sharp claws into Miss Milly's shoulder. At every attempt to dislodge her, she asserted herself with tooth and nail; having undoubtedly a claw hold, she would never resign.

This was Topsy's first claim on my mistress, and she made a slave of her ever after. All the family were pleased with Topsy. The advent of a coal-black cat into a family was looked upon as a very fortunate occurrence. Such cats have always been singled out from all others as associated with good luck. If one is driven from the house, it is thought to bring disaster.

In northern Europe the idea of prosperity is so associated with a black cat that the owner of a new house often sends a black cat there, before he takes possession, in order to secure good luck. The Egyptians called the cat "Pasht" (their name for the moon) because her eyes were bright in the dark. Of course I heard this from my mistress, and it is probably more interesting to me than to my readers. Miss Milly said Topsy had round yellow eyes, big enough to entitle her to the name of "Pasht."

She was so like Mrs. Stowe's Topsy in "Uncle Tom's Cabin" that no other name could be so appropriate. If standing on her head and fighting every thing that moved, even a leaf, could make her like Topsy, she deserved the name. She was full of life and electricity. If any one smoothed her fur the wrong way, in the dark, sparks would fly, and a snap like a fire-cracker would follow.

We have a picture of her taken with the two boys. Karl has a great sleepy creature called Daisy because he was white and black and had green eyes. He is, as usual, asleep on the boy's knees. Will holds Topsy, and his face wears a distressed expression, for she is tearing and clawing him, trying to escape.

Daisy belonged to Miss Eleanor. She brought him home one evening from a friend's. She put him in a closet over night, Karl slept in his aunt's bed, and just before morning she got Daisy and hid him at the foot of the bed.

When Karl awoke he teased for a story. Aunt Nellie bewitched the children with her original tales of animals. She began the oft-told story of the little pig family, when Karl said,—

"Hark! I hear breathing."

"Nonsense," said Aunt Nellie; "perhaps it is the little pink pig."

Pretty soon, however, the kitten had grown warm and comfortable, and ventured on a louder purr than he had given before. Karl started up saying:—

"Oh, stop! Aunt Nellie, I do bleevs it is a kitty."

There was no longer chance for concealment, and the kitten was produced, to the boy's great delight. When Willie came in from his mother's room to ask for his story, the same fun was repeated.

The children were very much pleased with him, and named him Daisy. Their aunties remonstrated at one of his sex being called Daisy; but when the children asked in an aggrieved manner, "Are there no boy daisies?" as they were not able to answer the question in a satisfactory manner, he was allowed to bear the name of Daisy. (There is no doubt that since then they have decided that boys have as good a right to be called Daisies as girls, for my mistress called me Daisy, and I like it.)

Three years after Daisy came to them he disappeared, and they mourned long for him, particularly because they thought a neighbor who disliked cats had killed him.

Topsy quarrelled with him and drove him about, but Daisy was sweet tempered and bore it so quietly that Topsy despised him. She did not love any cat unless she could fight with him. Topsy had a great many kittens. Like many human mothers, she was not fond of taking care of her children. She was very peremptory, cuffing them right and left at the least provocation. She was a cat "Mrs. Jellyby," the Borrioboola-gha mission being more to her taste than her home. She did not care to chaperon sons and daughters into society, and she cast them adrift as soon as possible. One kitten was always kept for her, and she never seemed to miss the others. When she was ready to wean that one, it was provided with a good home, without the least interest on her part. The family were very fond of kittens, but dared not get interested in them, for they could only keep two at one time.

She had one beautiful little black one, and Miss Eleanor became so fond of her that she decided to keep her for her own. She deserves another chapter.

X

LITTLE PEARL

LITTLE PEARL was coal-black, with one little white star under her chin. She was the only one of all Topsy's kittens that was black. Topsy did show more affection for her than for any of the others. She had bright yellow eyes like her mother's, and her fur was soft and glossy as silk. She was very sweet tempered, and never would strike back, as her brothers and sisters had done when their mother washed them, cuffing them if they dared move.

Miss Eleanor was devoted to little Pearl, but all her care could not keep her. She died from some internal disease when she was about four months old. She was a perfect skeleton, and her mother nursed her out of pity because she could not take much food.

One evening Miss Milly returned home from a visit, and on going to Miss Eleanor's room saw something in the middle of the floor covered with an apron. Miss Eleanor sat by the window, in great affliction. She lifted the apron, and there lay little Pearl, looking just like a lovely piece of sculpture.

Miss Eleanor said: "I had her in my lap, when Topsy came in, and as she seemed to be amiable, I laid little Pearl by the side of her. Topsy began to lick her fur, and then she allowed her to nurse. But it was only a feeble effort; her little lips fell away from her mother's breast, and with one soft sigh little Pearl's short life ended."

Topsy looked at her for one moment, then, with a piteous mew, she rushed out of the room and never returned till Miss Milly found her, and, taking her in her arms, comforted her.

They took a strong pasteboard box and laid in some wool and a soft handkerchief, and little Pearl looked lovely on the soft white bed. They put geraniums and white flowers around her; for she had played often in the fragrant beds they plucked them from. Then the box was closed up and put in a back room till morning. They made Topsy keep an unwilling vigil to keep away rats.

In the morning they engaged three children belonging to a poor family living near them to dig a grave. They came armed with shovels and spades enough to dig many miles. Miss Milly said she worked harder as overseer than she would at digging the grave alone. They were willing to work, but ignorant of the way.

It was a very pathetic sight,—a dark cloudy day, the sun obscured, the wind rustling through the trees, and even the flowers drooped their heads; Miss Eleanor, with the box in her arms, and Miss Milly with the improvised grave-diggers standing by the open grave.

Miss Milly held Topsy in her arms; but it was hard work, she made such frantic efforts to free herself. At last she did escape, and ran up the apple tree, and out on the branch that hung over the open grave. Here she looked down on them, while they laid away her dear little kitten.

After the grave-diggers had raked the earth over the spot, and received their money and departed, Miss Eleanor and Miss Milly put fresh flowers around it and a large pot containing a nice geranium in the middle.

Topsy had come down from her perch and roved about the garden as if possessed by an evil spirit. They had gone into the house but a short time, when she trampled all the flowers on the grave under her feet and knocked over the flower pot. Then she roved back and forth till she found a neighbor's cat, with whom she had a feud of long standing, and worked off all her sorrow in a free fight, where she proved the victor, and at night she returned to the house just as composed as usual. She never visited little Pearl's grave to their knowledge again.

The house where the family lived was large and old-fashioned,—one of the houses Salem was noted for at that time, long ago given up to the march of improvement. It belonged to a wealthy sea-captain in the India trade. Since his death it had not been cared for or repaired, and was therefore within the means of a small family. The remains of his extensive wine cellar consisted of a multitude of empty bottles.

Topsy was very fond of this cellar. They often remarked that she probably found kindred spirits of the past, for she always surprised them with some practical joke on her return to the upper regions.

One day, just at dusk a crash came that shook the house. The sound came from the cellar, and on taking a light there, they found the floor covered with bottles. Through some unknown agency, Topsy had moved a shelf, and all the bottles had fallen to the floor. There she sat on a barrel, looking on. If ever a cat delighted in a sensation, she did.

Quite a young girl lived with them, to help the girl of all work. She got the impression that the house was haunted. She said the doors would fly open without visible agency, and the bells all over the house would ring, and when she answered them, every one would be surprised; they had not touched them. They explained to her that the wind moved the old-fashioned latches, and the doors, being old, would fly open. Possibly rats would move the bell wires and make them ring. It is impossible to uproot a belief in the supernatural out of the mind of an ignorant child.

She said: "It is that black witch cat Topsy. She is an evil spirit. I shut her up at night in the kitchen, Molly says she never let her up; but there she is, upstairs, all over the house, during the night."

They could not persuade her to stay, and after she left the mystery was solved, as such mysteries almost always can be, in a very common, matter-of-fact manner. Miss Eleanor said at the time that she thought her room was the way Topsy came, though how, she could not say.

One night, about eleven o'clock, being very wakeful, she heard a slight scratching sound at the door. She sat up in bed and watched. She was not afraid, for she was sure the mystery was about to be solved. Another rattle of the latch, then the door opened wide, swinging back, with some long black thing hanging from the latch. It was Topsy. She had jumped up and knocked up the latch with her head, holding on the lower part with her paws, and in this way had entered the room every night.

Changes came to their home, and the death of their mother made a break in the household. They moved to Boston and were perplexed about Topsy. What could they do with a cat of her restless nature in a few rooms? What could she do without a large house and garden to roam about in, and, above all, how could she leave that cellar? The people who took the house were very anxious to keep her, and at last it was decided to leave her on trial.

Miss Milly said, "After what we have passed through, as we are breaking the last tie to home, one parting more we can bear."

After a few weeks Miss Eleanor went down to see about Topsy. She had a tale of woe to listen to. They said: "Topsy searched the house after you left, and at night she caterwauled in the hall in the most fearful manner, and paid not the least attention to us, when we tried to coax her. She refused all food, preferring to steal all that she wanted. She at last took to the cellar, and would not come up. We put food and drink for her every day, and it was gone, so we supposed she took it."

They said the night before she had made such a racket that it seemed as if there were a dozen cats with her. They had that day decided to write, asking what could be done with her.

When they opened the cellar door, and called her, no answer came; but the moment Miss Eleanor went to the door, and said, "Topsy," she flew up the stairs like lightning, and into Miss Eleanor's arms, just like a child. She held her so tight she could hardly remove her claws from her shoulder.

"This decides it. I shall have to take her," Miss Eleanor said; "and indeed I could not face Milly without her, now that we know how unhappy she has been."

They loaned her a shawl, and in it she wrapped Topsy, who followed every movement with her yellow eyes, though she kept as quiet as a lamb. Her trust was perfect; she knew she had found her own. She made no trouble on the journey by cars to Boston, keeping her eye on Miss Eleanor's face out of one corner of the shawl.

They were perfect slaves to her, keeping her in one room. Boarding was not very convenient, even with a quiet, well-behaved cat but with her it was a dreadful experience. She had come to Boston, a great and gay city, and she did mean to see the sights. The very first Sunday she crawled out of the window, though it was only open a very little; but she squeezed herself out on to the balcony that ran around several of the houses in that block, and Miss Milly went all over the street hunting for her. Being a stranger, it was very hard. At last Topsy was found on the balcony just outside the next house, all in a heap, and for once well frightened.

After Mrs. Rice and the boys came from the South, and they had a home, she was very happy, and it was then my mother met her, about which event I have already written.

I did pity them; at the last, to lose her in such a manner was very hard.

Miss Milly was so sad after this that Miss Eleanor said she hoped she would never tell Topsy's story again. Miss Milly would say, taking me in her arms, "I never felt comforted till I had my Daisy."

This pleased me, and made me very careful to do just as they told me to. I was very glad I had heard Topsy's story. My opinion is, that the witches wanted her and called her home. Very likely she rides on their shoulders when they go through the air on a broomstick.

XI

REMINISCENCES

I WAS suffering much from my shoulder just at this time, but we were very quiet, and I enjoyed lying on the lounge or in their laps and listening to the stories of the pets they had loved in their childhood. Miss Eleanor would read aloud, and indeed (you may laugh if you please) I could understand the nice things she selected.

One day she found some of Martin Luther's sayings. He one day remarked to his dog, that was growling, "Don't growl, little Hans, for in the resurrection thou, too, shalt have a little golden tail."

Miss Milly caught me up, saying, "Thou, too, Daisy, shalt go to heaven, and have golden bells on thy collar, for thy tail is more lovely than a golden one could be."

"How absurd you are!" said Miss Eleanor.

"Well, I do not think it absurd to believe we shall have our dear pets in the hereafter; heaven would not be heaven without them. God has not given them to us to love, without making provision for their hereafter. We have no little hands and feet waiting for us on the 'golden shore,' but little paws of all colors I know will be extended in welcome, and we shall be happy with our own again."

This comfortable doctrine suited me and made me very happy. Knowing that I could not live many years longer, the thought of an eternal separation from my loved ones would have been unbearable.

I did try to be good and be a comfort to them, but often my good resolutions were put to a hard test.

My mistress had one young friend who detested cats. She was very beautiful, and they loved her very much. She came to see us one day, and after greeting them affectionately, she said as her eye fell upon me, "Oh! have you got that old Tom cat now?"

How I bristled up! But Miss Milly was equal to her. "Would you like to have me speak of one of your children in this manner?" she said.

"I should think not," replied her friend; "but this is only a cat."

"And a cat that we both love as dearly as you love your children."

My rage at being called a "Tom cat" knew no bounds; it seemed to degrade me, and I thought to myself, "How can I avenge this insult?"

One can always find a chance to do wrong, and mine came at once. I espied her hat, gorgeous with feathers, birds, and wings, and brilliant beading. To my great discomfort—for it was very scratchy—I seated myself on the crown. I had no compunction when I heard the crunching of the beads and feathers, as I bent them under me. They seemed to say, "Tom cat,—indeed!"

I sat there till I felt pride had been sufficiently levelled; and as I chewed the delicate end of one of the expensive feathers, I felt that I might (in vulgar phrase) call myself even with her. Then I went under the bed, where I could with safety witness the impending tempest.

I was not disappointed. Words are powerless to express her wrath. Had her wishes been consulted, I should never have seen the light of another day.

When I saw how my mistress was distressed over my wickedness, my conscience did prick a little, though I did not repent. I had been called a "Tom cat," and for once I acted like one.

The climax was reached when Miss Eleanor produced a box containing a lovely wing and ornaments, and placed them where the broken ones had been. She said:—

"I do not approve of such decorations. Were I young, I would never wear anything that had been killed to pander to a foolish vanity. These were given me to put with some flowers and grasses for exhibition. If you will accept them in place of those our naughty pet has destroyed, I shall feel we have atoned for his thoughtlessness."

Accept! I guess she did, and in her heart thanked me for giving her such a treasure, though she gave me a cross look at parting, which I returned in full and longed to give her an etching.

I was disgusted. I had been outwitted, as people often are when they seek for revenge. It made me cynical, and I remained under the bed, thinking of the wrongs that are beyond redress, going on daily. I said to myself:—

"Just see! To gratify personal vanity how many millions of beautiful birds are slaughtered! Innocent creatures that God made, just like the lovely flowers, to make the world charming! And if a cat or any other animal kills a bird or chicken, their legitimate prey, knowing no better, they are called horrid creatures and hunted about just as if they were murderers."

They did not say anything about my naughty act; but I heard them (after they had called me to come out, and I had not answered) say, "Daisy is asleep." Then they laughed, while Miss Milly said: "Who could doubt that cats can understand, if they had seen Daisy's face when he was called a 'Tom cat.' I believe he sat on that hat to show his indignation."

All our friends were not of this order. One young artist was very fond of me, and we were quite chummy. He was a great big fellow, with a thick head of hair, and a mouth like a shoe-brush. I loved to see his teeth gleam through when he laughed, for they were perfect and white as snow. I did not like to have him rub his face over mine; it was like a porcupine, while my fur and whiskers are as soft as silk.

One day he had been fooling with me, and I gave him a good scratch. I raked his whiskers well, making his lip bleed. After that he called me his bar-ber-ous friend. Perhaps he thought I did not see the pun intended, but I did, and the point also.

I was rather sorry, and surprised. Somehow I thought his hair was like grass, and I could claw it as I pleased.

He brought me very nice catmint from his country home. Once he brought a pasteboard box with "Daisy" printed on the cover. I was very proud of that box, and always turned it over with the name

31

on the top. He brought us a beautiful pitcher called after the Emperor Hadrian. The style of pitcher was taken from those found in his tomb.

You will see I have a taste for history. There is no doubt, had I lived at that period, I should have made wonderful excavations. Mummied mice or rats would have had no mercy from my claws.

My special interest in this pitcher was the beautiful white daisies it was often filled with. The contrast with the blue pitcher was perfect. He would bring in a bunch from his country home, and say, "Here, Daisy, are your namesakes; they are for you," while I would pretend to smell of them, delighted to make them all laugh. I would mount the table, and lie down by the side of the pitcher very contented.

My friend went to Virginia to sketch. He wrote word that he had planted a large grove of catmint for me, and had called it "Daisy's Plantation." Was I not happy and important! As Miss Milly said, I was a real landowner.

After his return, he went to Germany to study. In all his letters he remembered me. I was just as much interested in his progress as his other friends were, and enjoyed the photographs of his pictures he sent home.

In my opinion he was a great artist—better than the "old masters" they talk so much about. The "young masters" are good enough for me. He wanted to paint my picture, but Miss Milly refused, just as she had all other offers of this kind.

I did not like it, for I thought my friend would do me justice, and it might make his fortune, if exhibited. I used to look in the glass and pose, thinking what a lovely picture I would make.

I say it, and I suppose you will say, "What a vain cat!" But how about these society women (and men, as to that) who dress in velvets and jewels, and exhibit their charms, and so much of them that it makes a modest cat blush? What if they don't say, as I do, that they would make a lovely picture, do they not act it? You will soon discover, if you never knew it before, as you read my history of many cats, that animals are often superior to the human race.

My mistresses would often dress me and make me pose to please them, and for the life of me I could not see why I should not be painted for the benefit of others. They would tie a half-handkerchief on my head, the point trimmed with lace just between my ears, the ends tied under my chin. They called it a "Marie Stuart point." Whatever that might be, I knew not. I afterward learned that she was a queen, and was executed. It pleased my cat vanity to represent a queen.

I myself performed all the tricks I could think of. One day, being in a large armchair, I just posed, myself. I sat down, hung my two paws over the arm of the chair, my head on one side, my "Marie Stuart point" all right, the bow tied under my chin, my collar and padlock in sight, and then and there I made an impression never to be forgotten by those who saw me. As long as memory lasts they will remember me in all my beauty.

My mistress fell on her knees beside me, calling me all the pet names she could think of, while Miss Eleanor said, "If ever a cat lived that could equal Daisy, that cat I would like to see!"

I remained a long time in the same attitude, proud of my success. When Miss Milly brought a little hand-glass for me to see myself, I did not wonder they were delighted, and I wished they would let me pose for the benefit of poor cats. I knew I could draw a crowd.

I never would pose for those I did not care for. I tore off the handkerchief as soon as they put it on, and taking it by the lace edge, I shut my teeth on it and dragged it under the bed. After this they only asked me to pose for my friends. For them I was very willing to do my best. I enjoyed being called a "darling" and a "love" by pretty girls, just as any boy would enjoy it.

One friend of my mistress, a charming little woman and a real philanthropist, was quite fond of me. She was the mother of my dear girl friend, whom I introduced to you at my party. This good little woman was a real friend to animals of all kinds, but she particularly loved cats.

She told us one day when she came to see us about the cruel people in her neighborhood who went away in summer, leaving their cats to starve. She said she had the past summer chloroformed eighteen cats in the last stage of starvation and too far gone to save.

She had two lovely cats named Chico and Sancho. They had very beautiful clear white fur and blue eyes. They were very bright, learning readily many little tricks. They would turn a graceful somersault for their food, and behaved at all times with great politeness.

Chico had trouble with his teeth, and Sancho was in great distress about it. This sympathy was almost human. When he found he could do no good, he retired in deep distress to the corner of the room, where he preserved a grave silence. The family dentist soon made matters right by extracting the troublesome teeth, making both cats very happy. No doubt Chico disliked him just as children dislike those who operate upon them, even though the kindness is evident.

Mrs. M. said, when she was telling my mistress about Chico, "Of course you will have Daisy's teeth filled with gold when they decay?"

"Certainly," Miss Milly replied; "and I would hold him while it was done."

For days after this I had no peace. Visions of doctors with horrid instruments were ever before my eyes. I shut my mouth tight when any one came in; and at the name of doctor I fled under the bed, where I remained with fear and trembling, fearing my teeth were to be operated upon. I could not clean and brush my teeth, but I got a bit of grass and one of my catmint stalks, and sharpened my teeth on them, keeping them as nice as possible, to preserve them.

Last year I lost one tooth. It fell out without any pain, and I did not miss it; but Miss Milly did feel so badly about it, and cried when one of the family said, "Daisy is quite old; it is the beginning of the end."

Miss Eleanor was very indignant, saying, "If it is not 'the beginning,' it is the end, of their visits here; we will not entertain such cruel people."

They were more careful of me than ever after this. They cut up my food very fine, and I was very careful not to gnaw meat off of a bone, for fear it would injure my teeth, and bring the "beginning of the end" after me. Whatever that might be I did not know; but it was such a scare to Miss Milly that I thought it must be some monster that would devour me as soon as I lost my teeth.

Our nice friend told us a great many stories about cats she had known and loved. Her charming daughter, my girl friend, could make cats perform tricks very easily. She seemed to charm them. There were photographs of cats taken in every position, and they seemed to do just as she wished, for she took the pictures of them herself.

We had very few cats in our neighborhood, and I did long sometimes to see one of my own old friends. I went out every day when it was pleasant, and sat upon a high fence, where I could look into back alleys, where the poor people had one or two miserable rooms, scanty furniture, and probably very little food, and I noticed with pleasure that in every one of these poor homes a cat could be seen sitting before the small fire, an honored member of the family. I wished I could write a check for these good-hearted people. It made me laugh; for who would honor a cat's check?

If I could talk, I know my dear friends would help them, if I could tell how much they need it; but as I cannot, I must content myself with good intentions.

XII
CAT TALES

THERE is no doubt that cat lovers will be interested in the true stories of cats that our friends related to us from time to time. I have them all in my memory. If they can arouse a love of cats in the hearts of my readers, this little work of love by one fortunate cat will accomplish its purpose.

Our friend told us a very wonderful story of a cat named Alexander. There seems to be a fitness in his name; for he was, in my opinion, very great. It does look a good deal like a "fish story," though I know it is strictly true; for he was a Boston cat, and lived not half a mile from our home.

Alexander was a prime favorite with all the family. He was the master's special friend and pet, while the mistress had a bird she was very fond of and had kept a great many years. Alexander had been taught to respect its rights, and ignored it as beneath his notice.

They had bought a beautiful house at the seashore, reached by the boats every hour or two from Boston. They closed their city house, and removed all the family, including dogs, bird, and last, but not least, Alexander, to their summer home quite early in the season. They went down by boat, and, as one would suppose, neither dog nor cat could well find his way back alone.

Alexander was taken in a large basket; one of the most reliable of the maids had charge of him, while the bird was taken by one of the family. Alexander had in every way protested against this move. He walked about the house, superintending the shutting up of rooms, with grave displeasure.

The dogs, bird, and family soon settled themselves, and the new place assumed an air altogether homelike. Alexander was restless and morose, and the third day he was missing. They had noticed the stolid air of disapproval with which he had gone around, looking with critical eye upon the house and its surroundings. He avoided the side of the house that faced the water, proving that he did not care for sea-bathing, and the air evidently did not agree with him.

They spared neither money nor trouble in searching for him. No clew whatever could be found, and they mourned him as dead. They returned early in September to their Boston home on account of illness in the family.

They had been at home only a few days, and the house had settled into that homelike air so pleasant to returned wanderers, when one day, while they were at dinner, Alexander walked in. He was the shadow of his former self, thin, rough, and gaunt looking, the very fierce expression of his eyes making him look like a stranger.

He refused every welcome extended to him, looking at them with disdain. He marched to a table, mounted it, gave one spring, and before they could realize his purpose he put his sharp claws through the cage door and killed the little pet bird.

He looked around upon them all with an expression of satisfaction, as if to say: "Now I am satisfied. You have enjoyed the company of your pets; you have not been satisfied with going away and leaving us in our good home, but you must have another. If the little fools you took with you were willing to stay, I was not. You left me to wander, and I have taken my revenge."

The mistress was very unhappy at the loss of her pet, and demanded Alexander's life in exchange—"a life for a life." Her husband refused. He sympathized with her loss, but he stood by Alexander. The master was the only one that cat would trust. He avoided all the other members of the family, and never recovered his cheerfulness or his good looks. The iron had entered into his soul.

Where he spent the summer months remains a mystery. From the change wrought in him, it could not have been in very elevating company. But the question is, Where did he spend that time, and how did he get back to the city? Is it not a convincing fact that cats know more than they are supposed to? And if they are such intelligent beings, ought they not to be treated with humanity?

It is true they will be hunted and abused by bad children; but properly taught, might they not be made nice playmates for children, even taking the place of a nurse maid if trained to do so? It does seem right for all animals to be studied and their good traits encouraged.

Horses have been, ever since the world was formed, the friend and patient slave of man. No animal has suffered more abuse patiently borne than the horse. And now that the fools of fashion have presumed to improve on their Maker's work, clipping them, cutting their tails, and using the abominable check-rein, they are objects of pity to every right-minded person.

My mistress had a friend who often called to take her to ride. She had been away, for a long time, travelling. On her return she came to see us, and asked my mistress to ride with her out into the country. We were very much pleased, for they both needed the air; and as she said she would take Miss Eleanor the next day (the carriage holding only two), there was a pleasant prospect for both of my dear friends, and I was delighted, for they had stitched and stitched till I was nearly frantic, looking at my sharp but useless claws.

I could only express my satisfaction by walking around her, and rubbing my head against her dress. She was quite pleased, saying, "Daisy has grown more lovely then ever," and she patted my head with such soft dogskin gloves, I did long to chew them.

As Miss Milly prepared for the ride, her friend said: "Just look at my new horses. Are they not beauties?"

"These are not your horses!" exclaimed Miss Milly, as she looked from the window.

"Certainly they are," her friend replied, "and I knew you would admire them."

"I am sorry to disappoint you," Miss Milly said, "but I do not admire, though I do pity these poor creatures. Is it possible that you had their tails cut in such an absurd manner? And their heads held up so cruelly?"

"Of course I did," replied her friend, while her face grew red with anger; "and I mean to have their heads raised an inch every day till they get used to it."

Miss Milly untied her bonnet, saying, "Much as I need a ride, I could never enjoy it, in sight of such cruel suffering. How could you do it? I thought you so kind-hearted, when we were girls together, that I cannot believe you have changed so sadly."

"How absurd you are! I think you carry your old-fashioned notions too far, and I must say you are very unkind to refuse to ride with me. Every one has these things done, why should not I?"

"You need not be cruel because others are; and I thought you had independence enough to do as you thought right, regardless of the weak and wicked who know not right from wrong. In your position, with wealth at your command, you could set an example that others would follow; for there are always those who are ready to do just as people in better circumstances than themselves are able to do, no matter what foolishness it leads to."

"I hope, Eleanor," said their friend as she turned away from Miss Milly, "you are not going to refuse to ride with me because my horses are in the fashion, we all know Milly is a crank on such subjects."

"And in this case, I fully indorse her," said Miss Eleanor. "It is cruel to cripple such noble creatures and make their lives a curse."

"Well," said the other, "I have had a lesson this morning." And tears of vexation stood in her eyes.

"My dear Laura," Miss Milly said, "just think that all we have said to you has been in kindness, because we believe in your real nature. Let your own heart speak for these poor creatures that cannot help themselves, so wholly in your power."

"And make myself a laughing-stock! No, thank you! I shall keep my horses like other people's. I am very sorry not to take you to ride; it is a real disappointment to me."

"It is an equal one to us. We fully appreciate your kindness in offering us a luxury beyond our means, here we recognize the Laura of bygone years. Come some day with 'Brown Bess,' the nice horse you used to drive, and we shall be glad to go with you."

Laura looked very red and confused, and replied, "We did not bring her to the city with us."

They learned some time after that the good old horse had been sold for a hack. My mistress was very indignant. She said she would have sold her own flesh and blood just as soon as a faithful old horse. She said, "If money hardens one's heart, as it has our friend's, we are better without it."

I mounted a chair and saw the carriage drive off, and I did pity the poor horses. The foam fell from their mouths, and they pranced and glared about in torture from which there was no escape. I was sorry my friends had lost their ride, but I was very glad they acted up to their principles.

I looked at the very pretty little woman, sitting so quietly in her carriage, and I said to myself, "If those poor tortured creatures should run away and injure her for life, could she complain? Do not animals have lessons of cruelty taught them every day? What reason have they for being better than their owners?"

I was sorry I had allowed her to pat my head. It brought on a fit of indigestion, and I left my nice kidney; I could not swallow it.

XIII
MY FIRST THEFT

PERHAPS a confession of my sin may be a warning to others. I know it will be interesting to my friends. It was in the house of the "philanthropist" of whom I have written before in my book.

One day when I went down for my outing I saw a door open that I had never noticed before. It is a well-known fact that a cat never passes an opening without looking in; they never leave a mystery unsolved if they can discover it.

The conditions were favorable, no one was about; "Oliver Twist" was out of the way; so I just wandered in. It proved to be the store-closet, and on a plate unfortunately near me, within my reach, was a piece of steak. It was large, but I saw my opportunity. It looked very nice, just like the steak our good doctor ordered for Mrs. Rice. She could taste but little, while I could devour it all. Thought I, "This will be nice for my mistress." So I just jumped up, and after several ineffectual efforts got it in my mouth. By holding my head high I could just walk with it, for it was long and reached to the floor.

It was some time before I could get started, for I was all of a quiver, starting at every sound, and in my hurry, tripping over it, getting so mad that I said, "Hiss! hiss!" just where an old boy of the human kind would have said something more to the point.

Then came the greatest difficulty,—three flights of stairs to mount. I had to rest at every landing, and when at last, breathing hard, but proud and happy, I laid my offering at my mistress's feet, instead of the delight I anticipated she screamed out, "Oh, Daisy, what have you done?" I looked at her, amazed. "You naughty cat! Look Eleanor," she said; "see! he has stolen this piece of meat. What shall we do?"

"I am very sorry. Of course we can pay for it," Miss Eleanor said, "but then Daisy has lost his character; they will never trust him again. Oh, how could you be so naughty, Daisy?"

I began to realize that my little offering had not been the success I thought it would be. Why, I could not understand; so I just walked under the bed, my place of refuge, and in high dudgeon reflected on my deed of darkness, for such it seemed to be. Miss Milly had scolded me, Miss Eleanor had reproved me, and I was very much provoked.

Miss Eleanor said: "I will go down and speak about it. If you go, you will be so provoked; if they speak one word against Daisy, you will not keep your temper."

I waited in fear and trembling, not knowing what would be done. She soon returned, saying, "I have paid her for half a pound of steak."

"Half?" said Miss Milly; "why, it could not be over a quarter, and old steak at that."

"I know that, but I would have no words with her. I simply told my story, expressed my regrets, and asked what I should pay her, and gave the money in silence and disgust. She remarked she always thought Daisy was a sly one."

This aroused a tempest of wrath. Having to pay twice the amount for a piece of stale meat was nothing compared to her calling me sly.

"Come out, Daisy," my mistress said; "I know you are sorry, and did not understand how wrong it was to take that steak!"

I did not go out for a long time. My feelings were hurt at the injustice I had suffered; and I was very dignified. My mistress took me in her arms, saying:—

"My dear kitty, I know you did not mean to do wrong; but to take anything belonging to others that is not given to you is stealing, and people are punished for it—I do believe," she said to Miss Eleanor, "that this dear cat got that steak as much for us as for himself." And she gave me a hug.

Then I could no longer control myself. I could not speak, but I got up and put both paws around Miss Milly's neck and licked her face. She was quite overcome, as she said: "I will never forget that you did this for me. But you now know what stealing means, and must never do it again."

And I never did. But oh, how good that steak did taste! I had heard it said that "stolen fruit is sweet," and I found it so. I had worked hard over it, and I enjoyed it.

I was not very unhappy that my mistress had to pay for it; for I had a friend who gave me pennies enough to buy all my extra food, and I said to myself, "She can take the money from that." So that afternoon I went to the table where my little tin bank was kept, and just pushed it off, and out came the pennies.

The noise aroused my mistress. How they did laugh, saying, "Daisy is paying for her meat." But they put them all back and kissed me, saying I was a very honorable cat. I wished I could speak and ask my mistress if that "philanthropist" was a church member. If so, did they allow extortion?

I think "Oliver Twist" was a free-thinker, for he seemed to grasp everything as his own, recognizing no law; certainly he did not favor our church. Perhaps, like the cat that a smart boy tried to sell, she represented the belief of the person to whom the boy offered her. When this enterprising boy had offered his cat to a member of every other denomination, he came to an Episcopalian. He was asked why he called her an Episcopalian, when he had just said she was a Baptist. "Oh," he answered, "but her eyes are open now."

I think "Oliver Twist" and his mistress were born with their eyes open.

This little item has run in my silly head ever since Miss Eleanor read it.

I must tell you before I forget it about the friend with the high-stepping horses. It was not quite six months after her visit to us that I wrote about that she was taken very ill and sent for my mistress to come and see her just before she died. She said to her:—

"Milly, I have never known one moment's peace since you gave me such a lesson on my cruelty to my horses. I seemed to realize, after you had spoken, just how foolish I had been in following a wicked fashion. My husband has promised me that Aunt Mary shall have them, and she is so devoted to animals she will never allow any abuse. Though I cannot restore their tails, they will be made comfortable. Old Mike, her coachman, will make them happy if any one can. I realize all they suffered, and think I deserve to lose all I misused so thoughtlessly."

Is not this an illustration of the good one brave word can do? If my mistress, fearing to offend her wealthy friend, had not spoken, the poor horses would never have been released from their suffering, and the conscience of her friend never awakened. If every one who is witness to an act of cruelty would remonstrate against it, there would be some chance of reform.

Many people say, "It is no business of mine if people ill-treat their own animals." But it is the business of every one with Christian feelings to speak for the poor dumb animals, for they cannot speak for themselves. Children, if taught when young, would never be cruel.

Miss Eleanor saw a little boy carry three little kittens into a lot where a house was being built. The boy was sent on this cruel errand by his mother. Their cries made Miss Eleanor's heart ache, and she had decided to go over for them and see what could be done to keep them, when a poor woman came along, who could not turn a deaf ear to their piteous cries, but went to them. They were so glad to see her, she said, though she was poor, she could not leave them alone. Miss Eleanor gave her some money, and the woman said she would find them good homes.

This is only one instance of what is going on day by day. Is there no help for it?

XIV

RELIGIOUS ASPIRATIONS

ONE ambition of my life has never been gratified. I have always had a desire to attend church. I have never been able to understand why restless children, who have no understanding of sermons, who are wretched when obliged to keep still, and are only kept quiet by a promise of something nice or a threat of punishment, should be taken to church and the family cat left at home.

What if we do sleep all through the service—we have a precedent for it. How often we hear people say, "Mr. So-and-So might as well have remained at home, for he slept all through the sermon," or, "Mrs. So-and-So had to pinch herself to keep awake. She dare not sleep, fearing to crush her new bonnet."

If we can believe all we hear, ministers all have voices "like old cows" or "dying calves." They never speak plain, and deaf people remain at home rather than look like fools when they cannot hear one word. Cats hear all these speeches, and wonder why they cannot go and judge for themselves. I know in our church, with the boy choir singing so lovely, one could not sleep.

When I was young I brooded over this question. I did want to be a Christian cat, and, like most ignorant people, I thought I could not be good unless I went to church. Of course I know better now. I can be just as good at home. Like all young things, I wanted to try my wings and see a little of the world.

Karl and Will were choir boys, and I was very proud of their voices. I did not understand why I could not march in the processional, right behind Karl and Will, even if my voice was not trained to sing.

I thought it all over, and out of a multitude of thoughts came forth an act. Not one of the "Acts of the Apostles." Had it been, I might have been successful.

One Sunday I made up my mind to try my luck. I had a hearty breakfast, washed myself all over, and cleaned my nails, for I had heard that "cleanliness is next to godliness." I did not mean that in my cat vocabulary there should be one such word as "fail."

I hid myself when Karl and Will were ready for church, and after they had left the house I crept out after them. I followed them on the opposite side of the street, without being discovered, when, just as I was feeling sure of the situation, a dog must needs bark and make for me.

Karl and Will turned around, and then my church-going was ended. Before I could run away Will caught me up in his arms and carried me home.

I was very angry over it, and refused to be comforted. I wished I had been a heathen; then they would have taken the trouble to convert me. I tried to find a rat to kill, and crept all around the cellar. But no; rats must not be killed on Sunday. I was very unhappy. Six days of the week I could do very well, but oh my, the seventh!

That day was a poser to me. All the family had gone to church. What could a poor cat do? I could not sleep, and, to cap the climax, a plate of beans and a saucer of milk had been put out for me, in case I wanted something before they returned.

Now I love my beans Saturday night and Sunday morning, but to be expected to make a dinner of them, in place of the nice little lamb kidney that was served up for me every Sunday, was adding insult to injury.

I dragged the beans out on the floor and threw over the milk saucer; then, as I could do no more mischief, off I went in a huff to look out for their return home.

I did feel a little ashamed, for I remembered that Karl could not get a kidney. The man at the store told him they were all sold, adding, "If that cat of yours will not feed on anything but kidneys, he will die of kidney disease." It was not their fault, and I did feel mean.

Every Sunday Karl and Will studied their lesson. They would sit at the table with their books, while I had a hassock in front of them, with my little Bible open on it. Here I would pose for an hour, with my paws folded on the open book, looking from one to the other, for I loved them dearly.

This Sunday I would not look at my book. The boys tried to make me, but were obliged to give it up. I behaved just like a bad boy, running after imaginary balls, jumping over the hassock, sitting on the Bible, till at last Will said: "I will call Aunt Milly. We shall never get our lesson if she does not take Daisy away."

This did not please me. I just picked up my book, and when my mistress came in I was sitting at my hassock, my claws clasped over my Bible (though it was upside down), looking as innocent as possible.

All this naughtiness because I wanted to be a choir boy and walk in the processional with the rest of the boys. I think it would have been better if they had taken me to church.

One thing always gave me great pleasure: I never could tire of cat stories. I think it may be a help to the understanding of cat nature if I give the most interesting ones for people to read.

With the horrors of vivisection and other cruelties practised upon animals, it is time for them to assert themselves. Even a cat's voice may be heard. Children can be taught to respect the rights of animals if their parents will interest themselves in their dumb servants.

My mistress met two very nice ladies one summer while in the country. They were cat-lovers, and gave many nice anecdotes of cats they had known. I will tell you one I particularly liked.

A friend of theirs had a great many cats, and as their number increased she felt the necessity of giving up some of them. She found homes for all but one; and one day, when her friends were visiting her, she asked them if they would take the cat and drop her near some nice house, where they had no doubt she would soon make a home. It was not a very pleasant commission, but they could not very well refuse.

Pussy had evidently heard their conversation, for she tried to hide from them. She was very quiet, never responding to their coaxing, covering her face with her paws in great sorrow. They drove many miles into the country before they could think of parting with her.

At last a large and finely situated farmhouse attracted them by its homelike aspect. It was a low, rambling house painted red, and the barns and outbuildings were in keeping. Everything looked inviting. The large kitchen-garden at the back of the house seemed just the place for cats to enjoy. An opening in the trees gave them a glimpse of a small stream meandering through the country, reflecting the rustic scene in its clear depth.

"Here," they said, "we will leave her. Surely no one in a place like this could turn away from a poor cat."

They coaxed her, and in spite of her clinging to them, put her down very gently. She stood like one dazed. Then she turned and surveyed the house and its surroundings. She looked long at the clear, bright water, as if in deep thought. She then looked up at the sky, and after giving them a reproachful glance, she walked slowly toward the river. Reaching it, she paused one moment, then deliberately walked in. Twice she rose to the surface, then the waters closed over her forever.

They could make no effort to save her. Knowing cats' strong dislike of water, they had no idea she would go near it. It was, they said, a clear case of suicide. Homeless, friendless, and wretched, she preferred death, even in the element a cat usually dreads, to seeking a new home.

The people were very unhappy about it. They said they felt like murderers, and never had believed before that cats could think and suffer. They said that they should ever after do all they could for animals, particularly cats, in atonement for their share, though unintentional, in the death of poor pussy.

It made me appreciate the care I had had all my life, when I heard such sad stories of cats.

Cats are fond of mischief, and I fear I never thought of the sorrow I should cause when I saw a good opportunity for fun.

We made a visit one summer in a family where the old grandfather, from Vermont, was spending a few weeks. He was an original character, and we were entertained by his quaint speeches and his old-fashioned manners. He thought Boston was one of the biggest and wickedest places in the world. I was the only one he seemed to be at home with, though I never could tell why, for I disliked him from the first sight I had of his horrid little eyes, with a real wicked expression, and his flesh looked just like an over-baked apple.

The wonder of all to me was his head, which was the part I could not understand. It was covered by uneven, red-brown hair, with no seam in it, and it looked just like a cocoanut.

He ate so loud I thought some one was choking, and when I walked over to the side of the table and looked in his face, I found he was eating with a big knife so fast it made me wink. This increased my dislike of him, and I refused all his overtures to make friends with me.

He said I was "a proud critter." He guessed lots of time was spent on keeping my fur so nice. And "as to that trinket on my neck, it was too fine for a cat."

One day I solved the mystery of his head-gear. I chanced to peep into his room,—as no place was sacred from my investigation,—and I saw another old man, his head as bare as the bed-post. When he said "Pussy, Pussy," I fled in alarm, but not before I had discovered that it was the same old man minus the top of his head. It was a wonder to me, and I never rested till I found that head-gear. They called it a wig, but I called it a "bird's nest."

Then I made up my mind to investigate it. Soon my opportunity came. All the people had gone to ride, and I was making a tour of the house, when loud breathing convinced me my old man was at home. Bad cat that I was, I just followed the noise, and sure enough, there he lay, flat on his back, his mouth wide open, sound asleep.

Of course I climbed up and looked into his open mouth. Another discovery I made: he had not one tooth in his head! And the wind and spray that covered me, from his open mouth, satisfied me with a brief investigation.

On the floor, by his side, lay the bone of contention, the brown wig I had speculated on so long. I grabbed it, and carrying it into a corner, inspected it thoroughly. Then I clawed it a little, and at last seated myself in it. Something about it acted like a narcotic, and in this uncomfortable bird's nest I fell asleep.

I dreamed that I was sitting under the piazza, when I heard voices. One of them said: "Why should not cat's fur be used for wigs and bangs? Gray hair is so fashionable."

"Oh," replied a young voice, "think of Aunt Sally with a maltese front-piece, and Grandpa and Uncle Jim with tiger-cat wigs!"

"Well," replied the first speaker, "if it were the fashion, we should like it. That great, pampered cat belonging to those two big-feeling old maids would make nice wigs, for his fur is as soft as silk."

41

"Yes, and that long tail of his," said the young girl, "would make a beautiful tippet, with a squirrel's head on it."

"But," lowering her voice, "if Brother Rob was here I would get him to coax him off, and get his skin. It would make a beautiful rug for my room."

Just then a shout awoke me, and the old man on the lounge also. He fought wildly for his wig. Dazed by my dream, I sat blinking my half-open eyes from one to the other. They were just screaming with laughter at the sight I presented, seated in Grandfather's wig.

Miss Milly took me out rather roughly, I thought, and smoothed it as well as she could. The old man looked on in surprise, muttering, "I knew that durned critter was up to mischief."

After it was combed out and put on right, the old man, conciliated by a good dinner that he loved, invited me to a seat on his knee in token of his forgiveness. I declined the favor with scorn. Sit on a knee covered with corduroy when all my life I had been used to broadcloth? Never!

My dream troubled me very much. I am a superstitious cat, and believe in warnings. So I kept close to my mistress; for in every one that approached I saw an enemy ready to despoil me of my beautiful fur coat. Though I am a good judge of human nature, as silent people are apt to be, I never had that confidence in people, that makes life so pleasant, I had felt before my dream.

When we left for home, Grandfather Tomkins said to Miss Milly: "You had better give that great critter to me. He would like my farm to run about in, and I have taken a liking to him." Then he added, with a sly wink at me, "He can sleep in an old wig I have at home."

I trembled at the thought, and hid in the folds of Miss Milly's dress, as she said, "Daisy is just like a child to us; we could never part with him."

"Well, well," he said; "I believe the critter knows all we say."

I was glad enough to see the last of that place. I preferred one room and no companions but my own friends. These uncongenial people had given me a good lesson.

I was more careful about running away, for when one has a fur garment to protect, suspecting every one of a desire to make wigs, front-pieces, tippets, and fur rugs of it, he has a great care. I only wish I could tell my dream to my friends, but it is a great consolation to write it.

XV

CAT ANECDOTES

I HAVE never been particularly fond of poetry; it has always, with a few exceptions, seemed to me to be "wishy-washy."

One day when it was quite dismal and rainy, Miss Eleanor said, "This little poem of Tupper's is a real protest for the future life and immortality of animals."

Of course that great big word was a poser, but after a time spent under the bed and a great deal of stuttering I mastered it. Then she read these lines, and I must quote them because they may influence those who never have any mind of their own, and depend on other people's opinions, to believe that cats have an after life.

"Are these then made in vain?Is man alone, of all the marvels of creative loveBlest with a scintillation of his essence?

"To say that God annihilated aughtWere to declare that in an unwise hourHe planned and made somewhat superfluous."

And then she read the story of the poor wretch whom no one followed to the grave but his faithful dog, who walked so mournfully behind the hearse.

Yes, I could understand and see it all, and when Miss Milly wiped her eyes, and Miss Eleanor's voice grew tremulous, I had to wink and sneeze several times to conceal from them how deeply I was touched.

And I know all that I care to about funerals. When I hear the roll of carriages, I mount a chair and look out of the window, and feel so sorry for them, remembering how I felt when they carried away our dear one, and left me alone all day, sitting in her easy-chair. And when I see that dreadful vehicle called a hearse, I am thankful that cats do not have to ride in them,—above all, the little white hearse. It does look just like the circus cars that I have seen pass, and the first time I saw it, I looked behind for the elephant, and the other beasts I had always seen in their train.

It makes one a convert to cremation. If I had the question to decide, it would be cremation for man and beast.

I hope women will excuse me for not mentioning them first. We fall into the bad habit of speaking of man only, as if men were the only ones worth a thought, but it is a question no one can answer, "Where would be the men, were there no women?"

I think the heathen custom of burning wives on the funeral pyres of their husbands a good one. It would certainly help dispose of some of the "surplus women" men are so exercised about; for if the widows were all disposed of, there would be a chance for the single ones. And if there were no divorces, no second marriages, then how careful husbands and wives would be of each other, if they knew the survivor would have to do escort duty on that last, long journey, to the one death had marked for its own.

Perhaps all this is too deep for a cat, you think. Well, perhaps it is; but then, cats can't help thinking of all the abuse heaped upon them and the unjust remarks on their habits and ways of living and having their children: and I ask, in the name of slandered cats, why is such judgment passed on them? They are not married, so are not unfaithful, and they are not divorced. While they live with another husband they have all the children that God allows them, and they take care of the little ones till they are of an age to look out for themselves.

Now I hope it will be handed down to posterity that one cat who has himself lived a blameless life has dared to compare the morality of cats with the morality of human beings, who are supposed to be so much more intelligent, and are bound by the laws of the land to be honest and virtuous.

Please don't say, "This cat knows too much," for I will tell you stories, and true ones, too, that will make you believe in the intelligence of our race. I feel sure my cat stories will be appreciated; for in a large company of strangers, where all are sitting around in grim silence, just let some one have the courage to tell a cat story, and the ice is broken at once. This "one touch of nature" makes them all grin. It is the "open sesame"; like a hydra with never ending heads—they spring up. As soon as one is finished, another begins. The heads all have tails (or tales) of cats they have known. One is surprised at the wonderful revelation of how deep a hold the household pet has in the hearts of those who love him.

My mistress had another story from the same lady who told her the last one I related. It was called, "A Confiding Cat." In 1877, says a writer in "Nature," "I was absent from Madras for two months, and left in my quarters three cats, one of which, an English tabby, was a very gentle cat, an affectionate creature. During my absence the quarters were occupied by two young gentlemen who delighted in teasing and frightening the cats. About one week before my return the English cat had kittens, which she carefully concealed behind the bookcase in the library. On the morning of my return I saw the cat and petted her as usual. Then I left the house for about one hour. On returning to dress, I found that the kittens were located in the corner of my dressing room, where previous broods had been deposited and nursed. On questioning the servant as to how they came there, he at once replied, 'Sir, the old cat, taking them one by one in her mouth, brought them in here.' In other words, the mother had carried them one by one in her mouth from the library to my dressing room, where they lay quite exposed."

I do not think I have heard of a more remarkable instance of reasoning and affectionate confidence than this in an animal. I need hardly say it gave me great pleasure. The train of reasoning seemed to be as follows: "Now that my master has returned, there is no risk of the kittens being injured by the two young savages in the house. So I will take them out for my protector to see and admire, and keep them in the corner where all my former children have been nursed in safety."

I think it a lovely story. Some will say, because the cat was an English tabby, "So English, you know!"—in a sarcastic manner; but I say as the old man did, "Nater is nater." And a true mother cat will fight for her own, whatever nation she belongs to. I wish all professional people were like this cat's master.

And I do think our colleges would do better to confer the degree of "B.A." on cats and dogs than on many of the brainless creatures made in the "image of their Maker." There is where the resemblance ceases, "image" is the only indication.

If some of the students would expand their hearts by defending poor abused animals, it would be much more for the benefit of society and for their own development than rowing and kicking as they do. They kick enough between the ages of one and ten to last a lifetime. And I would like to ask one question more, while I am about it: Is there one man, woman, or child who can play ball equal to a cat?

I hope the time will come when doctors will just as soon use the knife on their children as they now do on poor animals so completely in their power. I believe they will have to suffer for every case of cruelty offered up on the altar of that scapegoat called "science." God who made the victim will require atonement.

In my humble opinion, if all the stories told of them are true, it would be no loss to the world or their friends if science could be benefited by the cutting up of a few doctors' and ministers' children. Perhaps by exposing their hearts (while they suffer the agony that poor animals do while under these operations) they might get at the root of wickedness and hardness of heart that seems to be inborn in them; and thus improve the morality of the coming generation. It would be no loss to society to sacrifice a few of them.

I can tell all the professors, and possessors too, that there is no earthly use in using a cat's or dog's heart or liver to decide what causes diseases in human beings. They are no more alike than fire and water. The hearts of human beings are not enlarged by kindness, and are hard from their own wicked natures, while their livers would be well enough if they indulged in proper food and drinks.

A cat's heart is tender and kind and gives love for love; and her liver—well, that is all right; she probably keeps that in good repair by a moderate diet of liver. And if a cat should have disease of the kidneys, why, "a hair of the same dog"—you know the old saying—will cure it, and a good diet of kidney will counteract the disease.

Of course doctors would scorn such a suggestion from a cat; but it might work in the case of their patient as well as in animals—only a doctor who dares order the plebeian diet of liver or kidney would never prosper unless he gave a foreign name to them or smothered them with a title. But just think of it. Do you often hear of the poor laborer with either of these diseases? He has liver instead of turkey, and kidney instead of chickens, and if he is not killed by some modern improvement, he is likely to live forever.

I offer this without the least expectation of a fee. I am no M.D. or D.D. I am "a Daisy"; but my eyes are open, and although I have green around me I am white. So if any one says in a sarcastic manner, "she's a daisy," I shall not be green enough to take it to myself in their sense, but just remember that "it takes a rogue to catch a rogue," and feel happy in my superiority.

While I am moralizing I might as well give my readers the benefit of it. Why are not cats used as barometers? It would certainly save much money, and Blue Hill Observatory would be a good outlook for the weather-wise cat, and she would make an able assistant without a salary. Just observe her movements as the earlier generations did, and there is no doubt the weather notes will be correct.

As early as 1643 an old book was published which says of the cat: "She useth to wash her face with her feet, which she licketh, and moisteneth with her tongue. And it is observed by some, that if she put her feet beyond the crown of her head, in this kind of washing, it is a sign of rain." If a cat scratches the furniture or frisks around more than usual, she is said to be "raising the wind."

Cats are sensitive to air, full of motion and electricity, which seems to put them in good spirits; while a warm lifeless atmosphere makes them languid.

Sailors are as a class very superstitious in regard to cats. Their family, when the father, son, or brother has gone on a voyage, watch the family cat to know about the absent one. If a cat sickens or disappears, it is looked upon as an indication of the illness or death of the absent one. A sailor's family will make a pet and companion of the family cat. The cat that chances to go to sea is just worshipped by all on board the ship and is the real captain.

There is another little story that comes to my mind just now, as illustrating how much a cat notices and remembers. The cat in question was called Ole. Why, or wherefore, I cannot say. Perhaps he was a Norwegian, from the name, or his ancestors may have been Norwegians. He lived in Syracuse, New York, perhaps he was named for that most perfect musician and gentleman, Ole Bull, as people have a craze for naming their children for celebrated people, and they often name their pets for them. There is no doubt that animals do greater credit to their names than pampered children.

The cat called Ole was a great favorite in the family where he belonged. He had his place at the table and was very fond of his master, following his every movement when carving, with great interest. Even though he craved what was being carved, he never made a movement to hasten his dinner. Subsequent events proved he had not watched in vain.

One day the daughter of the family was attracted to the dining room by the loud and peremptory calls of Ole. She opened the door, and there sat Ole in his master's place at the head of the table. The large mat for the meat platter to rest on he had drawn in front of him, and on it lay a large rat.

The satisfaction with which he greeted her was evident, and he purred forth his delight at having provided and served up a game dinner. It proved that he had thought about the etiquette of the table. Having no platter, he had taken the next best thing, the mat, where the platter usually rested.

It is needless to say Ole was more petted then ever, though people, when told the story, would say, "How wonderful!" but behind their backs would say they guessed it was a fish instead of a rat that Ole had caught. But I believe in the rat. A cat detects and despises shams.

A friend of my mistress said that in a country house where she was visiting they had an open fireplace in one of the rooms, and one of those very absurd gas-logs.

The family cat walked in one day, and, going over to the rug, prepared to have a delightful snooze. But she no sooner approached the fireplace than the idea of the sham fire arrested her. She gave one resentful look at her mistress and walked out of the room. She never went into that room again, preferring the reality of the kitchen fire to an elegant sham. There is very little danger that a cat will ever be deceived after she has had the chance to investigate.

If the ravens and birds were half as bright as Pussy, the best gotten-up scarecrow in the field would never cause them one moment of disquiet or the loss of one good meal. She has such quick ears that even the moving of a leaf in the wind or the creak of a window is enough to bring her to her feet ready for an encounter.

XVI
CAT PRANKS

WHAT pleasant memories I have of my early years! How could I be other than a very happy cat, with a home so pleasant, and dear, kind friends? With the boys to play with, and everything to interest me, I have nothing but loving words to say on my own account, and I feel more anxious to try to help the cats who are not appreciated to homes and friends like mine.

With all my advantages, I must admit I was at times a great trial to those who loved me. If a boy had behaved as I did, it would have been called the "old Adam" in him. And with me I suppose it was the cat old Adam. I was full of life and fun, and a great hunter of everything that moved, from a leaf that rustled in the breeze to our natural enemy, a mouse.

I was very smart at the business of hunting, and the rats and mice that I destroyed I cannot tell. I wish I had kept an account, but when young I did not know the value of a journal and account book. It would be a real pleasure to me now, when memory is often treacherous.

I was never allowed to worry or torment them, though I had the desire, as every one has, to torment or worry something. Miss Eleanor would put her hand around my throat gently, but it would force open my mouth, making me drop my victim. Then it was at once killed.

One day I chased one under the bed. I knew it had received its death-blow, and I wanted to go in and worry it occasionally. My mistress did not know of it; she was not in the room at the time.

It was just about tea time, and I expected a scene when it should crawl out, as I feared it would. It was behind a box, and I could not move it or get at it with my paws; but I scratched on it with my claws to assure it of my presence and make it tremble. In this way I kept it all the evening, and I did dread their going to bed. I was so sleepy, it made me cross. They went to bed, and I fell asleep with a guilty conscience, for I knew it would be a dreadful fright to them if the mouse should appear.

It must have been the middle of the night when a loud scream awoke me, and they both rushed out of the bedroom, saying, "It is a mouse! It walked over the bed!" Before they lighted the gas I had pounced upon my prey and finished it.

Miss Eleanor took a cloth and pulled the mouse out of my mouth and threw it out of the window. I was real mad with them both, and got up on the table, where I never was allowed to sit, and knocked down a beautiful little basket that Miss Milly kept flosses in. The three parts of the basket separated, and all the little bags and balls rolled about on the floor. I poked them under chairs and in corners, and at last my mistresses were obliged to go to bed, leaving me with my playthings. The moonlight favored me, and I not only chased the bags and balls, but I tried to chase the moonbeams. I caught the playthings, but never the moonbeams, and I wondered why.

The next day they talked seriously to me, but I did not care one bit. I washed my face all the time they were talking, and ran under the bed when they wanted to comb me. I chewed the red bow they had tied on my collar till it was black, and it tasted horrid. They did not scold me, for they were afraid I had poisoned myself with the red dye.

Miss Eleanor found in her book an antidote, and Miss Milly gave me the dose. She had a hard time of it, for I spit out the pellets as fast as she gave them to me. That did provoke her, for I knew how to swallow them as well as a child would know. She took me, and, opening my mouth, she dropped them down my throat and held my mouth till they were down. I coughed and fought to get them up, but it was of no use. When Miss Milly was determined on a thing it just had to be done.

I lived through that scare, and have chewed ribbons of all colors since then without harm except to the ribbon. It was very naughty, I know; but if I got mad, I would chew up my ribbon to provoke them.

Another wickedness to record. Like all young cats, I loved to run away. This was before I was stolen that Christmas time I have already written of. Every day I would go out in the yard and hide, and I now remember with great thankfulness how wonderfully I was spared. Poor cats disappear, leaving no trace behind, and I am fortunate not to have been one of them, and I understand why my mistress was afraid to trust me out of her sight. I would hide on the ledge of the fence in the next yard and then peep over to hear them call me.

They would scrape two knives together to call me in to dinner, when we were visiting or when we had the range of the house. Of course I responded promptly to the call, as cats, like children, are always ready for a square meal. But of late I had discovered their little game. There was no dinner; they scraped knives to get me in. They deceived me at first, but not for long.

Now the back of the houses on our street faced the back of the houses on the next street, with a long alley between. At the windows of the opposite houses there were young men who were interested spectators of this little by-play. Very soon they were not content to be only lookers-on; they wanted to take part, and soon they appeared with knives, and then a fearful scraping was heard, and the cries of "Daisy, Daisy" resounded through the alley.

I never turned my head or let them know that I noticed them, for I was very much ashamed of the sensation I had caused, and I crawled home, crestfallen enough, to meet the reproachful glances of my dear friends. They had not dared to appear on the scene. After that I went home without being called.

I was more provoked because these were the very young men who had thrown bottles, old boots, and bootjacks at the cats that assemble nightly to talk over their trials and give an open-air concert occasionally. Were these young men asleep as they ought to be, not just returning at midnight from some junket, they would be willing to believe in the doctrine of "live and let live."

These cats have no homes, no nice beds, and often they have empty stomachs; and if they console themselves with a social meeting, and end in a musicale, who can blame them? They certainly do not have empty bottles to dispose of after their meetings, as these young people do; and there is no uncertain note in their voices when they let it swell out on the midnight air. If it reaches a high C, it is not a "high seas over," as the young men's voices often indicate.

Another proof of the superiority of the animal over the human race. A cat may often be sitting on a beer barrel, but there never was a cat known to have the contents of one inside.

There are many shams in the world that cats would scorn to practise. Now I am, perhaps, about to shock some people by airing my opinion on "family worship." I can hear you say, "How irreverent!" Not at all. Just please read the many so-called bright speeches of children in the newspapers, where they hob-nob with their Maker just as if he were a boon companion.

I have heard my mistress quote, "Thou shalt not take the name of the Lord thy God in vain." I never have, and it makes me shudder to hear children so flippant with the sacred name. And I will never believe that cats or dogs could be taught (even if they had the gift of speech) to be profane, as the poor parrot is. They have an evil eye, and may not be to blame.

One year we boarded in a real country farmhouse,—at least, the master was a farmer; but the family were trying to find some more genteel name for the business and the place that had so long supported them.

It was a nice, old, rambling house, with quaint little nooks and angles where I could hide. The kitchen was very large and low, and the outbuildings so ample that I often lost myself.

The hay-loft was very bewildering, and after I had once climbed up I felt like the travellers my mistress loved to read of—very proud of my exploits.

They had a great yellow cat called Tabby. Now I did hate yellow, and of all weak names I think "Tabby" the weakest. But oh my! "What's in a name?" Sure enough, she was just the reverse of her name. Although she was not "my style," I could not, in that lonesome place, afford to pass her over.

After a time she became quite friendly with me, though at first she had resented my style, as she called it. She evidently thought I was a cat "Astor or Vanderbilt," with my collar and padlock,—that "bete noir" to all cats that I met. They confounded it with the ropes of pearls and strings of diamonds that society women pawn their souls for; but when I explained to her that it was an inexpensive badge, with the name engraved on it so that my friends could recover me when I got lost,—that it represented their affection instead of their dollars,—she, like a sensible cat, realized at once its use, and admired it, saying it was very becoming to the aristocratic bend of my neck. After this I did think she was a cat with good judgment and exquisite taste.

When she saw how delighted I was with her kittens, she allowed me to play with them all I cared to. They were all colors, and the loveliest little creatures I ever saw—four of them. They looked upon me in the light of a bachelor uncle, and were after me all the time. They grudged me the night separation, for my mistress would not allow me out of her room at night.

I was very clumsy with them at first, as old bachelors naturally are, but soon took them in my arms as deftly as their mother did. I was delighted to have them run after me and kick and bite me. I felt sad at first that I was denied this pleasure, that no little ones of my own would ever play about me. But, when Tabby told me her sad tale, I no longer regretted I had been spared so much sorrow.

She said when she saw them happy and loving to all around, she trembled, for she knew at any moment they might be taken from her. She said she had tried to hide her other kittens in every corner she could find, but it was of no use; they were all sacrificed.

They were delighted to play with my collar and padlock, and they scratched it so badly that my mistress said that if I was going to allow myself to be used by the "Scratch Grabble" family as a plate for their etchings that I had better go without a collar.

Go without my collar! Perish the thought! I would tie a blade of grass around my neck rather than go undecorated. Daisy without a collar! The idea!

The family allowed Tabby to go out and in as she pleased. She had plenty of food, and was treated kindly for her usefulness, for the rats she had killed counted into the hundreds; but petting was beyond their comprehension.

The father of the family was a big, jolly old man. His only fault was his piety. Now do not misunderstand this remark, for I have been brought up to respect true religion, but I do hate bigotry.

The farmer's wife was a large, red-faced woman, and very nervous and fussy. Her husband said, "Marier wanted to be a big bug." This gave the true key to her aim in life. She wanted to be fashionable.

They had only two children. The elaborate headstones in the neighboring cemetery where I had rambled gave the names of several children they had buried. And after I had known them a little while I believed, with Tabby, that the best part of the family were represented by the tomb-stones. They fought with each other continually, and their chief fights were during family worship.

The girl, Bessie, was fourteen years old, very fat, big-eyed, big-lipped, with tousled head; always in one's way, and disagreeable in the extreme.

The boy of twelve, red-headed, freckled, and full of mischief, was much better than his sister. Bob, as he was called, had one marked individuality—that was his appetite. I never saw that boy without his mouth full, and his pockets were a storehouse to draw from.

Their table manners were dreadful. As there were only two other boarders besides ourselves, the family were all at the table, and we had a chance to see them in all their glory. The food was of the best and well cooked; but oh, the way it was eaten!

The breakfasts were enough to make any cat sick; for when the last mouthful was swallowed, a greasy, ragged Bible was produced. As my friends said, though they did not approve of the manner in which it was conducted, they did not think it right to turn away from family prayer, and of course I remained with them and rather enjoyed it.

The daughter was made, by the payment of a weekly sum, to read the Bible. She gabbled off a chapter taken from any part of the book she chanced to open to first.

Bob was making faces and kicking her all the time under the table. Once in a while his father would take him by the ear, but not often. A loud yell of "Lemme alone!" was not a pleasant accompaniment to a Bible reading.

Then the father made a prayer. It certainly was only for his own benefit, for no one could distinguish one word he said. Then the children, after a long wrangle, engaged in a boxing match, the father and mother taking no notice of them unless called upon by one or the other to decide their dispute. It was very embarrassing to all but those concerned, and the boarders very gladly returned to their rooms.

Just as it was getting furious and exciting, my mistress took me away. She said she did not care to have me demoralized; but I was provoked, for I wanted to know who was the victor.

They were very much disgusted with the whole performance. Miss Eleanor said, "Why cannot people read one nice selection for the day, and a short prayer that will comprise all that one need ask for, instead of making such wretched exhibitions as we have just witnessed?" And we all agreed with her.

It seems an insult to one's Maker to gabble over prayers, with one's mouth full of food. It seems much more appropriate to ask a blessing before one sits down to the table than after.

It seemed to me real fun, a family circus; but then, I respected my friends' opinions, and knew that their view of the situation was right. I told Tabby what I thought of it, and she said, "It is a long time since I have attended their family prayers, and I will never listen to them again."

One morning she said: "Bessie and Bob had a fierce battle at prayer time, interrupting their father several times. When he had finished, he cuffed them both, and it ended in a real row. Then the mistress, who never could be just to any one, provoked with her husband for punishing the children, and angry with them herself, turned her wrath on me.

"'It is time Tabby's kittens were disposed of,' she said.

"'Yes,' the children yelled; 'lemme, lemme do it!'

"But the father interposed, saying, 'No cruelty shall be practised in my house.'

"Oh, how frantically I tried to claw open the door and get at my kittens! Not that I could save them, but perhaps they would kill me with them.

"The master took me and shut me into the closet, where I fell down broken-hearted. I mewed and mewed, for I knew I should never see my dear ones again. I could not sleep, my breasts ached from the milk that belonged to the poor little victims, and I spent the most wretched day of my life.

"Early in the afternoon Biddy, the servant, released me. She looked very sorrowful at me, and tried to make me eat some dinner, giving me a nice plateful. I could not swallow, and went out to the barn, though I well knew I should not find my children.

"A feeble mew greeted me, and I found, in place of my five beautiful kittens, only one. They said the prettiest, but they were all lovely to me.

"She was a light gray and bright as a button. She was so glad to see me, but looked surprised, as if she thought I would bring her brothers and sisters with me.

"I lay down exhausted, while she nursed, and I could feel the four little lips (that were now cold and stiff) on my breasts, and I felt too wretched to live.

"I was in a real fever for several days, but she nursed me all she could, and I got better. She was soon bright and happy, frisking about, and grew large and very handsome. I did not take any comfort in her, for I knew she would soon be taken from me, and a hard life begin for her.

"Can you wonder that after that morning's experience I never wanted to hear of family worship? If it does not teach them humanity, what is it good for? And if, as they read, God is so mindful of the sparrows, why don't he remember poor cats? Tell me that, will you?"

I did not answer her, my heart was so sad, and I wished I could speak and ask my mistress that same question. I comforted poor Tabby all I could. I said perhaps God lets these people do these things for an example to others. She scoffed at the idea as she asked, "Why did he make us?" As I could not tell, I answered meekly, "I do not know."

I expected every day these innocent creatures would go. Oh, how I did feel! Rash thoughts of taking them and hiding them in Miss Milly's trunk, filled my mind. I wanted to save them.

"There is no use," Tabby said, "we cannot fight against the mighty. All that I can do is to make all the noise I can in the world. I join all the cats around and speak in all the meetings. 'Anarchists' probably they would call us, but we do not care. We caterwaul and scratch and steal, just as human beings in our situation would take to drink. And I would ask, who is to blame? We did not learn this of animals. We learned it of Bessie and Bob and the good, pious people where we live."

I found I could do no good. Tabby was an eloquent speaker when the wrongs of her race inspired her tongue; and my heart beat, and my claws went out and in as I longed to fight for our down-trodden race. The whole barn would have been a battle-field strewn with the bodies of rats, could I just at this moment have encountered them.

When we left this place, my mistress said: "We will never go to a good quiet place again. We will take our chances with the multitude." I fully indorsed this resolution. This experience had made me a more thoughtful and a sadder cat, for the sorrows of animals preyed upon me. Had not the thought of writing this book entered into my mind, thereby opening the eyes of the thoughtless, and helping expose the wrongs of our race, I could not have existed.

How I hated to leave the dear little kittens, they were so fond of me, and ran after me when my mistress took me in her arms to carry me away. The woman told them that they were all promised to friends. They would have good homes; that was why she had kept them so long.

Miss Eleanor talked to her beautifully about their duties to dumb animals, but I knew it would do her no good.

After we were in the carriage, Miss Milly said she felt very sad to leave such dear little playful creatures, particularly as I had taken such a liking to them. She said she could not bear to think that they would go into new homes and be tormented by bad children.

Miss Eleanor said she had often seen children squeeze kittens, their soft little bones almost crushed, in their strong hands; and if they dare scratch or bite in self-defence, they were called bad-tempered and abused.

"There is nothing we can do to help them," they said, "but speak for them when we can, and always save them from cruel hands when we can do so. It is the duty of every man, woman, and child to speak for the dumb animals who cannot defend themselves."

I did not wonder Tabby was hopeless when Miss Milly said she saw no chance for cats or dogs either. If people who profess to love them are afraid to speak up for them, what is to be done?

Dogs and cats are not always enemies. They can be taught each other's rights, if their owners will take a little trouble. I will give you an illustration in favor of this theory.

A friend of ours owned a little dog named Friskey, and a cat she called Flossy, because she had soft fur, like silk.

They were very fond of each other. Flossy would lie down with her head on Friskey, making a pillow of him.

Their mistress taught him to beg for food; and after watching him awhile, Flossy took her place by his side, assumed just the same position, and begged.

They were very good to each other about sharing their food, furnishing an example children would do well to imitate.

They were both of them fond of candy, and one day their stock had melted away, and only one little sugar ball was left. It was very hard. They had each tried to break it, but finding that impossible, they took turns in sucking it. Friskey would wait patiently till Flossy had sucked it till she was tired, then he would take his turn, while she would rest and watch him with a happy expression on her face, saying plainly, "Is it not nice?" They licked and licked, but it did not seem to grow "beautifully less," and lasted them nearly one week.

They used it as a ball, and would run after it and then refresh themselves with a lick or two and then start again. Their owner said it was the most ludicrous sight she ever witnessed, they were so happy with their ball.

The mistress said one morning Friskey was in great tribulation, hunting for their ball of candy. Flossy hung around her, mewing till she got out her work-basket. Then Flossy made one dive and clawed out from the midst of cottons and silks the beloved ball. Friskey barked and wagged his tail, while Flossy licked it, and then gave it to him. She said the inside of her basket was rather sticky, and she told Flossy she must find some other hiding-place.

At last, that ball was reduced to such a sharp skeleton of its former self that fearing they would choke over it, she took it away and gave them some fresh candy. But she said: "One day, they had a gumdrop, and Friskey could not get it off his teeth, they were buried so deep in it; but Flossy licked and clawed till she got it off. That beat all the other pranks."

Now, how long would two children have kept that ball of candy? I would like to ask. If their teeth had not demolished it the first hour, the family hatchet would have been used, and a free fight have followed, over the fragments.

Friskey would lie down, and his master would put Flossy in his arms just like a child. They were very devoted to each other, though Friskey did not like other cats, and was very jealous of Flossy. He seemed to wish her to have no friend but himself. As she was a social little creature, and a "cat flirt," he had many heart-burnings.

Friskey came to a sad end. He was run over by a fast team and had to be chloroformed. Flossy was very unhappy about him. They said she acted just like a widow, and, probably, like most widows, got another admirer in his place. He was buried down in the garden quite a little distance from the house, and Flossy was often seen sitting on his grave.

The family thought it very pathetic, but there were others, people who like to destroy our best illusions (whom no one likes or cares for their opinions), who suggested an explanation of the interesting fact, by saying that a catmint bed was on each side of Friskey's grave, and Flossy went there for the catmint.

I do, for my part, hate to be disenchanted when I have indulged in a little bit of sentiment. I do not believe any one ever thanks the person who turns the poetry of life into prose.

My solution of the story is, that Flossy had often played with Friskey in that very catmint bed, and she went there to recall pleasant memories. I have a right to my own opinion, and I know I am very strange; but then, it would be a very stupid world if there were no variety.

I had a singular thought the other day, and it will do no harm to tell it, though I do not care one pin whether others agree with me or not. I think my mistress is original, and I know I am like her. My idea is this: I have heard the stories of Adam and Eve and Noah's Ark—indeed, I was brought up on Bible stories.

Now my thought is this: When Adam and Eve left the garden of Eden, there were two of their dumb companions whose hearts were sad for their master and mistress. They said, "We will not let them go alone." And when Adam and Eve left the garden, a dog walked by his master's side, and a cat by the side of the mistress—faithful in their misfortune.

XVII

THE STORY OF FREIDA

MY mistress was not silly about me. She would say: "I am perfectly satisfied with Daisy, just as God made him. I do not presume to improve what he has made perfect. I do all I can to bring out his good points, and leave the rest to nature."

Then she told me the story of "Adonis." His mistress had his ears pierced and gold earrings put in them. He wore them at home only.

That cat did suffer for his mistress's vanity, and I could not help wishing she had been the victim; for one day a lady called, bringing with her a pet dog. She said, "My dog has a lovely disposition, and will not touch your cat."

She had not calculated on Adonis having a temper, and the consequences were disastrous. Ever since his ears were pierced, Adonis had been fretful and snappish. His beautiful earrings were no pleasure to him, for he could not give them a pull without making his ears sore.

When he saw this pampered dog in his very home, he arose in his anger, and flew at the little pet in great wrath. Of course the dog retaliated, though frightened almost out of his skin. The result was, he tore out one of Adonis's earrings, making a long slit in his ear, and got repaid by having his own eyes almost scratched out.

His mistress was well paid for her cruelty in decorating her cat in this foolish manner. From a loving, happy cat he was transformed into a cross, quarrelsome creature that no one could love.

Then she cast him off and got a new plaything, this time a dog, all covered with bells and ribbons, that she could take around with her.

Poor Adonis was suffered in the house, but left to the servants, and his nice quarters given to the dog, while he was left in the kitchen, where his high temper made him disliked, and his torn and swollen ears made him an object of derision.

My mistress would say: "Never, Daisy, shall you be made miserable by such foolishness. People who treat animals in this way are not their real friends; they use them selfishly as a decoration for themselves when they might make them intelligent companions and sincere friends."

That there are many good people who appreciate animals, the stories that I have given you will prove. The story of Freida is an instance, and I can vouch for its truth.

Freida was a nice cat, aristocratic and refined in her ideas. She inherited her name from a Danish relative of her master, and brought the old home days back to memory.

She had a very beautiful home not many miles from Boston. It was a large house, and was called "The Mansion." It had a cupola where Freida could go up and overlook the high hills and see the gilded dome of the State House quite plainly.

Then there was the stable, and a beautiful flowerbed in front of the house.

It was rightly called "The Mansion," for it stood alone, surrounded by beautiful trees, and looked down with dignity on the smaller houses around it.

Freida was a very happy and fortunate cat. She had a kind master, and her mistress was very lovely and good. She was a very dear friend of Miss Milly, and was born in good old Salem, and, like all the people in that bewitching place, she thought a home was not perfect without the family cat.

All this would have been very delightful, had not a great change taken place in this charming home. But then, there would have been no story; for Freida's life would have been just like that of other cats, pleasant but uneventful.

The good mistress fell ill and was ordered a change of air, and a voyage to Europe.

I know how I felt, for I wanted my mistress to go abroad; and when her friend sent her a card decorated with wild flowers and edelweiss from Chamonix, I was just crazy to see this beautiful place that she wrote about so charmingly.

I was very wicked, I fear, for I got the card off of the table and sat upon it. I said to myself, "It is just as nice to sit upon the picture flowers as it would be to have the real ones." I thought how nice it would be to go with my mistress, for I was sure she would take me with her, and then I could run up and down the mountains just as I pleased.

When she took me on her lap, showing me the card, and told me how many miles of ocean separated her from her friend, it made me shiver at the thought of crossing it. But then, in her arms I would not be afraid to go to Jericho. I do hate water; there is too much used on me when I am washed, and I wish I could be washed with land instead.

All this is not telling about Freida, whose story I started to tell you.

The beautiful house was closed, and Freida was taken to the home of her mistress's brother near Boston. Two of her sisters, who were very fond of Freida, were there, making it homelike for her. But for all their petting she was homesick. They were obliged to keep her very close, for fear she would run away.

She was a great care to them, and one day they missed her, and on going to the furnace they saw a strange sight. A fluffy ball was turning over and over in the ashes, and on drawing it out they found it was Freida. She was almost suffocated, but the master, a charming man, just like his sister in kindness of heart, went at once for a doctor. He said they must take her where the air could blow over her, and also give her brandy.

Her tongue was hanging out of her mouth, and she was a wretched creature. They worked over her for hours, and then the sisters brushed off the ashes and tended her as kindly as they would a baby. Soon she looked as nice as ever, and that cat never tried cremation again.

It proves how good and kind people can be to their dumb friends.

Poor Freida! she was destined to die in a violent manner. She returned to her beautiful home only to meet her fate.

The man who carried groceries to the house had a very gentle and kind horse. Strange to say, a friendship sprang up between Freida and this nice horse. She was always on hand to greet him every day, rubbing against his legs and showing her fondness for him in many ways, while he would put down his head for her to caress. It was a very funny sight.

One day when the man came out he turned the wagon quickly, and it crushed over poor Freida, breaking her back and killing her instantly. The man was very much troubled about it, and he said, after that, the horse would try not to go up the hill.

She was buried near the place where she was killed, and they all mourned for her, and still remember her with affection.

They have a cat now called Frity, a dignified creature, but no cat will ever take Freida's place.

My mistress said that when she was visiting there she felt as if Freida's spirit was around, and at night she could hear her voice mingling with the voices of the pines.

How much sorrow we could save our friends if we could speak! People think cats cannot understand and read character, but they can; and they know the true from the false very quickly.

We had rooms, at one time, where everything was satisfactory, and the landlady said she was very fond of cats; for my mistress would tell the people of whom she engaged rooms about me.

This woman was very nice to me before my mistress, but I could not like her at all. And my instinct was right, for when I went through her kitchen, to go out for my daily airing, she looked "daggers" at me, and said, "Scat!"

I was so provoked I walked just as slow as I could and held up my head; but she came at me with her dishcloth, and as I did not care to be hit by that dirty thing, smelling of fish, I swallowed my pride and ran away. She slammed the back door after me, and called me a "pampered brute."

I dared not show my head again for a long time. I was cold and hungry, but I had faith. I knew I should be looked for; and, sure enough, both of them came to hunt for me, the woman of the house with them, all smiles. She said: "Poor Pussy! Did it want to come in?"

I just glared at her. I wanted to say, "It did not want you to let it in." I thought the treatment bad enough; but to be called it broke the back of my belief in her.

I kept out of her way; but one morning she saw me coming in from the kitchen, and drove me upstairs with her duster. My mistress saw her, and was very indignant, though she did not say anything, but she never let me go down alone after that.

This woman had a little step-son. She kept him in from play with his friends on Saturday afternoons, to get his Sunday-school lessons, and he just hated her and the lessons, as a matter of course.

I used to play and chase my tail as if I did not know what it was, to divert his attention, for I did pity him. He was pleased, but it made him forget the long, tiresome answers. So I gave up trying to amuse him, for I did not want him to be punished. And when, after all my sympathy, he pulled and pinched my tail, I said, "He is a chip from the old block," and left him to his deceitful step-mother.

I felt very glad that, with all their sorrows and wrongs, cats never have step-fathers or mothers. It is better never to have known your own father than to have one who is always bringing you a new mother. And I guess, after all, there is just as much morality among cats as there is among human beings.

Sometimes there were days when I could not contain myself. I wanted to run and fight, and send forth my voice just as other cats were allowed to. The Bohemian blood my poor mother suffered from was answerable for this state of feeling.

At this time we lived in a flat on the fifth story of a very high building. It was a very small place, but we were passing through sad reverses just then, though I could not understand, else I would never have added to their trials.

Miss Milly would go away every day, and when she returned at night, looked so white and tired, it made me very anxious. Though she petted me, and called me her greatest comfort, she did not play with me, and her brightness was gone.

After she had gone in the morning, Miss Eleanor and I would go about and attend to our little work, and then, when she would sit down to mend the boys' clothes, she would take me in her lap and talk to me about their troubles.

The boys had both found places, and were working very hard and away all day.

We were lonesome. The kitchen had a large window, and outside there was a long wooden box made on it, and here the janitor brought fresh earth every few days, for it was my garden park and hunting ground. It was my only outing, for I never went down over the stairs. When I went out there, I was so near the sky that the earth seemed very far away. I did long for a run over the green grass.

Miss Eleanor, when it was pleasant, would take me up through a boxed-up stairway to the top of the house, where I could run a long time. It was very large, for the building covered a great space, and was gravelled over like the street. A very high wall surrounded it, so there was no chance to run away.

One night I could not sleep. I was possessed to go out. The window of our bedroom was open, and I got out into the gutter and walked along. It ran around the building and was very narrow, and I half drew back. Then I said, "Courage!" and went on till I reached the corner where the pointed tower cut me off. Then I realized my situation. I could not turn around in this narrow space, and I closed my eyes in horror. I dared not look below, the distance was so great. Above, the beautiful stars seemed to look down on me and my wickedness.

How sorry I was! No one could see me, a little gray speck, way up so high. I remained there till the morning light gave me a little courage. I tried to think of good things, and I remembered about the little sparrows that God cared for, and I trusted he would not let me "fall to the ground" for my dear mistress's sake.

She had suffered so much I did not want her to have the pain of losing me. So I just shut my eyes and turned very slowly and painfully, with many slips and strains; but my face at last was turned homeward. Then I cowered down with real vertigo. I could not take one step; but soon I braced up and crawled along till I reached the bedroom window, where I was safe.

The delight of my friends may be imagined. They had hunted everywhere for me, and Miss Milly had had almost a nervous fit, for she said: "He has fallen down and has been dashed to pieces by this time." They did not go to bed, and were waiting for the morning light to search the building.

Of course I was very much ashamed, though it proved how much they loved me. I promised myself I would never try them again; and I was frightened when I realized what a narrow escape I had had.

Then I enjoyed my good breakfast, washed myself thoroughly, and getting into my nice basket, slept all day.

But there are moments now when the horror of my situation overpowers me, and I always hear with pity about the men who mount the high buildings and church steeples. And I never, though I am a patriotic cat, desire to go to the top of Bunker Hill Monument. The picture of it satisfies me. It makes my head spin, and I have vertigo of the mind; just to think of it makes me lose my head. For a cat to lose his head is a serious matter. We might spare a piece of tail, but we need every bit of the head.

That reminds me of a cat of Miss Eleanor that really lost half of its tail. Her name was "Persimmon."

The family all laughed at Miss Eleanor for her romantic idea, and very soon the name degenerated into "Sim"—a much more appropriate one for the wild and homely creature who answered to it. She was one of Miss Eleanor's many pensioners. Somehow the mean-looking and abused always were those she selected for pets.

After they had in vain tried to find a home for Sim, she at last settled down as one of the family, to the disgust of their old and well-bred cat.

Sim had no manners, and was not in the least degree sensitive. She was a dirty white, with pale greenish eyes; and a dark shadow under them gave her a weird aspect. Miss Milly said the dark shadow was "ashes," but Miss Eleanor said it was the "shadow of deep thought." More people, however, believed in the ashes than in the thought.

She would crowd herself in where there was no room for her; and after the loss of her tail, she was more determined to assert her position than before.

It happened in this wise: Sim had a very high temper, and in a quarrel with a bigger cat than herself she was vanquished. In trying to run away she climbed the fence. The cat following could only reach her tail. It was a long one, and she struck her claws into it with such force that she nearly tore it off. Sim went about, for a few days, a sorry object, till it fell off. The remains of it only measured about two inches.

She exhibited herself on the front doorstep whenever any one called, in an unblushing manner. A friend of my mistresses, a professor of music, asked what kind of animal she was, saying he had never met just her like.

At last she made herself so disagreeable that the mother said they must dispose of her. They felt badly, but their mother's decision they never questioned.

Sim was put into a bag and given to two boys of kind and reliable natures, who promised to care for her very kindly. She was taken to the Juniper, and drowned. The boys said they would take a boat out into deep water and drop her in. The society with the long name had not then been organized, and dear good Dr. Angell had not entered upon his life-long work of protecting animals, so this method of getting rid of them was thought the most humane.

The children had been sent to Beverly, to their elder sister's, to spend the day, and their mother hoped by her cheerfulness to make them forget the cat.

About five o'clock they returned home, and on going into the sitting room who should they see but Sim, or Bobtail, as she was called, sitting by the fire, washing her face.

Their mother laughed at their surprise. She said the cat was taken away at ten o'clock, and at four she saw a shadow on the window and heard a loud mew, and on her opening the door, Sim walked in. She fed her, and since then she had spent the time washing herself—a thing she never was willing to do.

It was too late, however, for her to reform. The mother had decided on her fate, and she was doomed.

"I shall see the next time that it is a sure thing," their mother said; "as to her return, we must investigate that matter."

Later on, the boys came in. They were not told of Sim's return. They were not exactly untruthful about it, but evaded the true story. They said, when asked how far out they had taken her, that they could not get a boat, and had got rid of her on the rocks.

"Are you sure she is dead?" asked the girls.

"Dead? I guess so! Dead enough!" they both answered.

"Then here is an instance of one returned from the dead," said Miss Eleanor, bringing in Sim, who yelled and scratched as soon as she saw her would-be executioners.

Their faces were a study. "Is it Sim?" they asked in such real astonishment that no one could doubt them.

"Now, boys," the mother said, "you have deceived us; but we will listen to your story if you will tell the truth."

With shamefacedness they said they did not mean to be deceitful; they really believed she was dead. They took her down to Juniper, and while they were trying to find a boat she had burst open the bag and run off over the rocks. They followed her, and she disappeared under a rock into the water. They heard a splash, and waited some time to make sure that she was gone. It must have been a stone that fell in, while Sim escaped. They were very honest in telling their story, and they were forgiven and received their money, though the mother decided to attend to the business in her own way.

When, some days after, Sim was missing, no one asked any questions, believing that everything had been done for the best.

But how that cat found her way home is a question no one could ever answer. The boys carried her down in a wagon. The Juniper (now called the "Willows"—a famous Salem resort) was about a mile from the home she was taken from. It is a rather crooked road for one to remember. She probably hid herself and followed the boys at a distance. My opinion is that Sim just used her wits, and thought it out as we all do, and followed the trail of the wagon.

It is really a cat tail we are all sure of.

The family said that they never could go down to that pleasant resort, in after years, without thinking that Sim was hovering around in spirit. Had she been black, a witch cat, they would have felt sure of it.

XVIII
THANKSGIVING

I SUPPOSE I am growing old and forgetful, for memory brings things to me upside down, as I have heard old people say. All I can do about it is to tell the little incidents relating to the past as they come back to me.

For the last few days Thanksgiving has been in my mind more or less all the time, and I think you will be interested if I tell you about one that I enjoyed very much.

My mistress took me in her arms one day, saying, "Daisy, you are going to have a real Thanksgiving."

I opened my eyes wide (I know that I have very handsome eyes, and love to show them off, just as boys and girls do); for I did not know what a thanksgiving meant.

"Yes," she said, "I have just received a note from our friend, Miss W. You know her." (I winked in answer, for I did admire her.) "Every year she sends us a turkey, with a basket of goodies all cooked, ready to eat. This note tells me that she will send the basket Thursday morning. Now you do not understand what 'Thanksgiving' means, and I will explain it to you."

I settled myself comfortably on her lap; she always put on a clean white apron to keep the hairs from my coat off of her dress. I resented this, for I could not see, for the life of me, why cats' hair was not quite as good as camels' hair that her dress was made of. And I just crawled under her apron one day when she was reading, and I liked the feeling of the soft wool better than I did the cambric apron, it was so woolly and warm.

I had just snoozed off, dreaming that I was asleep between the camel's humps she had told me of, when all at once she dropped her book, saying, "Oh, Daisy, just look at my dress!" And sure enough, it was covered all over with gray hair, for I was shedding my fur fast.

I was really ashamed of myself, and said: "I am just like Dr. Jekyl and Mr. Hyde. So I will just go under the bed, the best place for a 'Hyde,' and repent of my wickedness. I do not know why I do these things, but my mistress loves me all the same."

So this afternoon I sat on her nice apron, listening to her story of Thanksgiving like a well-behaved cat.

This is what she told me: That on the last Thursday of November it usually occurred. The Governor of the State made a proclamation, which was read in all the churches and published in the papers. The day was set apart for giving thanks for all the blessings God had bestowed on us during the year.

Of course I had to listen to all this, but I was awful anxious for her to get to that basket. But for once she was very tiresome, and now I am glad she was, for I have an idea of Thanksgiving I shall never forget.

Once, she said, people invited all their family, no matter how many or how poor they were, to dine. They always attended church, and then returned to a bountiful dinner of turkey, chickens, plum puddings of mammoth size, and pies of every variety. All the poor of the family would eat all they could for the present, and then fill in for the future.

The children, who never get too much, had nuts and candy in plenty, and the day was altogether lovely to them all, more particularly to those who gave than to those who received.

Now, she said, things were changed. No one invited or thought of the poor of the family, and no one went to church but the poor relations who had nowhere else to go.

Perhaps the minister preached from the text, "In my Father's house are many mansions;" that is, if he had an idea of the fitness of things,—that it would give the poor homeless ones a sure hope of the future, where perhaps those who have such nice homes here would not be as well off as the poor would be; and this Christian thought would help them bear their slights with patience.

Meanwhile the rich do not go to church. They give dinner parties to those who have money and a higher rank in society; and if one thought is given to their own flesh and blood who are poor, they wish that all the old grandfathers and grandmothers, uncles and aunts and cousins were old turkeys and chickens; then their necks would be wrung, and they would be rid of them forever, and would never be called upon to remember kindness rendered to them in the past by these same old relatives.

The sons of the family celebrate the day by a grand carousal, which leaves its mark on them for many days.

"But," she said, "we have no such days to remember, we are very quiet and sad, but very thankful for all our blessings; and you are one of the greatest. I have told you all this because I know you understand it, and I love to talk to you." (Oh my! how my heart did swell with pride when she said that.) "I want you to have a lovely time this year—a real Thanksgiving."

Of course I was all ready for it. I did not sleep much that night, and was early at the window to see the arrival of that basket. Long before it arrived I had thought long and seriously of all my mistress had told me.

I was perfectly wild when that basket came and they unfolded the turkey. I could have hugged him at once, he did smell so good, but I never moved from the hassock where my mistress placed me.

I never saw such a lot of nice dishes and beautiful things on them. Even the dessert had not been forgotten. There was such a big bunch of celery. I thought it was a tree, and that I could run up in it.

At last, after the inward cravings after that fowl had torn me almost to pieces, and my desire to be polite and good had been almost upset by the inclination to rush in and devour right and left, they carved up the turkey, and I had so many tidbits I did not know which to eat first, the head or the tail, for I had both of them.

I did do justice to that dinner, and, like a child, as I did not know when to leave off, they had to take it from me. I then laid down and slept so sound that I had the nightmare. I thought I was beset by poor relations: that an aunt was sitting on my head, an uncle on my tail, and cousins on my stomach, and they pressed me so hard that I yelled out loudly.

Miss Eleanor came to me, saying, "What is the matter?" Of course I could not tell her, but I did not want to have such visitors again. I would rather give them my dinner.

We had a very light supper, and my mistress promised me the sequel to my Thanksgiving the next day. Indeed, the sequel beat the beginning, and I thought how nice it would be always to live on sequels.

They took a big platter, and stood it on a newspaper on the floor. In it was the carcass of the turkey and all the giblets. Miss Milly said I should, for once, have a real low-minded junket.

And I did. It was like a bone-yard, with the remains all around me. I felt so generous that I would willingly have said "come" to all the poor relations in the world. They would be welcome to all the bones I had picked and all of the quack. It was lovely, but I was greased from head to foot. When tired, I seated myself on the bones, in the midst of the carcass, and my fur was glued together in places.

The work of cleaning me was something fearful. I was as patient as I could be, though I could not help jerking away a few times. Miss Milly said, "You do not look like my lovely Daisy," and it was many days before I looked like myself again.

That evening my mistress let me look at the photograph of our nice young friend. I thought it lovely and a very good likeness. I gave a little purr at it, but I suppose a gobble or a crow would have been more appropriate.

She is a very dear friend to my mistress, and I am very fond of her. When she comes in, I always keep awake to hear her talk. She is very fascinating. I do not think she cares very much for cats. I suppose it is because she does not know much about them. One thing I do know: she would be kind to them, for when I am left alone with her, she smiles at me and says, "Daisy, you are a nice cat," just the same as if my mistress were here.

Some people make so much of me before my mistress, but behind her back say, "Scat, you old cat!" There is no need for them to speak. I know them, and would not go near them on any account. Then I do wish I could speak and warn my mistress of their falseness.

One of these people called one day and brought her great boy with her. He could hardly keep his hands off of me. When my mistress took his mother into the next room, to show her some work, he lingered behind, thinking, "Now is my opportunity."

He pulled my ear and yelled "Sassage meat" in it. Whatever he meant by his "sassage meat" I did not know, but I saw my opportunity and gave him a good dig with my claws and made his cheek bleed. He bellowed well, like a real calf, and his mother looked daggers at me, for I boldly stood my ground. I would not go to my retreat under the bed, for I was not to blame.

Miss Milly was very sorry, and helped his mother wash his cheek and got court-plaster for her. After he had been coaxed and comforted, he poured forth his wrongs, saying that he was sitting quietly, when I rushed upon him and without the least provocation clawed his face.

Miss Eleanor came forward then, saying, "You are mistaken. I was in the alcove, and saw you pull Daisy's ear and yell 'sassage meat' in it, and he scratched you in self-defence." The mother was very indignant. She said, "I have always told Harold never to touch such spiteful creatures as cats." No one answered her, and she soon left with her pretty boy, and she never came again.

Miss Eleanor said she thought, as Harold was to be a lawyer,—so his mother had told her,—he would never let truth stand in his way in gaining a case.

My ear did burn from the sharp nails he had pinched it with, and I was not sorry that I defended myself, and I made up my mind that when children came to the house, particularly if they were with their parents, I would keep out of their way.

Miss Milly came to the same conclusion. She said: "Daisy shall not be subjected to a trial of this kind again; it spoils his temper and makes him rude, and then he is unhappy about it."

And I was. I had reason to remember it, for my ear was swollen, and they were obliged to put salve on it to make it heal.

Some time after this we went into the country for a short time. While there I made the acquaintance of a very intelligent cat. His name was Pedro. He was very hard to get acquainted with at first, and I was just wild to know him, for he was very handsome and dignified.

I thought of every reason why he was so cool to me. At last I said to myself: "It is my collar and padlock. He thinks I am proud." So I worked and worked till I got the padlock up on my back, and then I licked down my fur to cover my collar. Then I walked out, and after a few turns in the garden I saw Pedro on the grounds. He belonged to a very wealthy man, and the house and grounds were quite lovely.

I walked to meet him very humbly. When I said, "Good morning, Pedro," he looked me all over, and instead of answering me, he said with a scoff, "Oh, you are in disgrace, are you?"

"No indeed," I answered; "what makes you think so?"

"Because you are not in full dress, and I miss that trinket you are so proud of."

This did provoke me, and I said, "The 'trinket,' as you call my nice padlock, is on my back. I supposed it was that that made you so against me. All the cats are envious and jealous of that."

"Envious! jealous!" he hissed. "I guess I am not a mean fellow enough to be jealous of a trumpery bit of finery on a stuck-up cat."

I had to swallow to keep down my temper. As I did want his friendship, I passed over his insolence in silence.

As I turned to go home I said: "I cannot understand why you dislike me; I have been anxious to be friends with you, and have wondered if my collar and padlock had made you think I put on airs. I tried to hide this gift of my dear mistress, though it seemed treachery to her, thinking perhaps you would then be pleased with me. Now, of course, I shall never try for your friendship again."

He had been silent, but he moved about uneasily. Then he winked very fast, and at last said: "Is that really so? Did you want to be friends with me? Why, I thought of all the blue-bloodedest, old-familiest, aristocratical creeters, you were the biggest. I thought you were a cat duke or a count, and them's the creeters I despise, for I am a real democrat."

"So am I," I joyfully said, too much delighted to notice Pedro's bad grammar. "There is my paw on it, and I do hope we shall be good friends. We ought to be fast friends. As for the dukes and counts, I spell them without capitals. That is how I value them. The only likeness they have to us is that we have whiskers, with this difference: the barber makes theirs, while God made ours."

We laughed and had a jolly time over the dukes and the counts; the rest of the rabble we did not give even a small-lettered title to.

After this we met every day, and our friendship increased till Pedro confided his history to me. If ever a cat had cause to mistrust the whole world, he had, and my heart ached with pity.

It was one very pleasant morning when we had met and walked down and seated ourselves on a nice grassy mound at the end of the garden, that Pedro said, "If you would like to hear my story, I will tell it to you this morning."

Of course I expressed my pleasure, and, making myself comfortable, I prepared to give my best interest to the story.

"My mother was born in New York. While quite a small kitten she was given a nice home with people who believe that no home is complete without the family cat. She was a very large cat, striped like a tiger, with a beautiful long tail. She was amiable and affectionate.

"The people were very kind to her, and she was quite happy. They were not very wealthy, but they had great expectations. An old uncle, a very Crœsus, owned the estate they lived on, and a magnificent one adjoining, where he lived with a widowed sister. He was a childless widower, and made no secret of his intentions in regard to them.

"Of course they were not sure of his millions. He had given them a life interest, but should the children offend him, he would wash his hands of them at once. He was a rough, irascible, outspoken old man, despising shams, and a falsehood he would never forgive. He was a tender-hearted friend to animals, but his special favorites were cats.

"He was very fond of my mother, and she returned his affection. Tige, as she was called from her beautiful stripes, would run to meet him when he came to the house, walking very proudly by his side. He always noticed her kittens, always taking one for his own, while he would see that the rest were disposed of in a humane manner.

"When I was born, he made me his favorite. There were three besides myself, and we were called a very handsome family. My little brothers and sister were to be kept. Some friends of the family, who were cat lovers, were to have them, while I was to be the pet of my mother's old friend.

"My mother enjoyed us, for she was allowed to nurse us all till we were old enough to be weaned. Three of them were striped like my mother. I alone was Maltese. Probably I favored my father; never having seen him, I cannot tell.

"It was the first of July, and two of the boys belonging to the house were at home on a vacation. They were not bad boys, but were full of life. Boys will be boys, you know. They had been kind to my mother, though rather rough, and she kept her kittens out of their reach.

"We all found them changed for the worse, and I was sorry they had a long vacation. They were never still. They drove the pony in a reckless manner, and gave the poor dogs no rest.

"Tige, my mother, had always been a favorite; now, though they seemed fond of her, they were teaching her tricks all the time, making her jump over strings and hoops when she was sleepy and did not want to be troubled. And then they would take up the kittens by the tails, to hear them squeal, saying, when their mother remonstrated, that it did not hurt them.

"But I can tell you it did hurt. Imagine being taken up by the feet, the blood rushing to the head, and then put down with a jerk, while everything would look dark around, as the blood, in flowing back, seemed to settle around the eyes. It was fearful suffering, and we did squeal well. They were never caught by the uncle in such pranks, you may be sure; they were too sly.

"My mother dreaded them and would hide us the best she could under her fur. She had no peace, for her anxiety made her afraid to leave us alone long enough to get her dinner. I know it all now, but then we were so young we did not care for anything except to cuddle up together and see which one could get the most milk out of our mother.

"The boys were to have two cousins to spend the Fourth of July with them. We could hear, from our nice basket home, all about the great preparations the boys were making to celebrate the day. All the young people living in the homes near were invited, and the uncle had spent no end of money in fireworks and Chinese lanterns and all the things boys love.

"He said, 'This is the one day of the year when children should be made happy, and they will be more likely to remember its meaning.'

"The two cousins who came were disagreeable-looking boys. All the animals on the place, from the horses and dogs down to my mother, instinctively distrusted them, for animals find out their enemies very quickly. They soon found they would have no peace while these boys were here, for the visitors were not afraid of the uncle.

"I cannot tell you the horror of the night before the Fourth of July. The boys were out till very late, and by five o'clock were again on their feet. The yelling, blowing of horns, and firing of crackers made us almost crazy. My mother would jump at every fresh noise, for, like all cats, she was of a very nervous temperament. I now believe she had a presentiment of coming events.

"We could not get one square meal. Just as we would get our lips on her breast, ready for a good mouthful, she would jump and jerk away from us; and as we had no teeth, we could not hold on;

besides, the worry and fright prevented the milk from coming. My poor mother, how she suffered that night!"

Pedro paused, overcome by his feelings, while I ventured a word of sympathy.

"We had been removed from the house into one of the outbuildings, quite a good distance from where the fireworks were to be, close to the stable; and we enjoyed seeing the horses and pony come out to the great trough to drink. It was exactly opposite where we were, and was very cool, the drop by drop sounding very soothing, though we did not exactly like the water. Our removal had been the work of our kind friend, the uncle. He knew, however delightful the noise was to young America, that we did not enjoy it at all.

"All day they were around the grounds with their crackers and pistols, and the din and smell of powder made all the animals in the stable wretched; but my poor mother suffered more than all the others, with four refractory kittens to care for.

"The family had a great supper, and then, about eight o'clock, the fireworks began. They were a great success, and when nothing was left but crackers, the elder people went into the house, where the windows opening on the veranda gave them a fine view of the grounds.

"The old uncle had entered with boyish delight into all the fun, and was supposed by the boys to be in the house resting. There was a ripple of excitement as some of the boys left the fireworks to the younger ones, and stole away, as they thought, unnoticed.

"One of the cousins, a great big fellow of sixteen or seventeen, came, and taking the basket containing my mother and her four little kittens, carried it out of the shed, and put it on a rock by the side of the pump. Next, he took some straw and stuffed it in all around the sides of the basket. From behind a hedge one of the boys got a can and handed it to him, and from it he poured kerosene over the straw and all over the sides of the basket.

"I saw all this with wonder. When he took up the basket, I was hanging over the side, and fell out just before he put it down. He had not missed me, and my mother was probably so frightened and choked by the smell of the kerosene that she could not think. I was quite pleased with my liberty, though I did not know how much it would influence my fate.

"Before my mother could start up and try to remove her kittens a tramp of feet made her aware that her tormentors were approaching. She could have jumped and saved herself, but, like a true mother, she cowered down over her kittens.

"The boys were all in high glee, while the big fellow yelled out, 'Here we are, and we will show you a piece not on the bill.'

"Quick as thought he applied a match to the basket in front, while another great fellow held a burning paper to the straw at the back of the basket, and all fell back as a loud report was heard, and a volume of flames sprang up around the basket."

Poor Pedro paused, overcome for a moment, while I almost gasped for breath, soon he continued in a trembling voice:—

"One shrill scream from my mother, and the last sight I had of her was in the midst of the flames, her fur all ablaze, her eyes starting from her head, and magnified to three times her size, while three little flames around her repeated the dreadful picture in her three kittens.

64

"A fearful oath rent the air, and powerful hands cleared a passage and seized the basket and plunged it into the trough that chanced to be filled to the brim with water, and held it there till the flames died out, and the last sobbing breath was still forever.

"The flames had enveloped his arms, his sleeves were burned to flinders, and his hands were a fearful sight. But to me his face looked like the face of an angel, and I crawled up on his boot, with one little mew. He heard it, and in spite of his maimed hands took me up and dropped me into the pocket of his loose coat, where I knew nothing more, for my little brain was dazed at the fearful sight I had been witness to.

"He was a profane man, and they said the air was blue with the language he used. Doctor L., his great friend and physician, chanced to be near. He said, 'My dear friend, you must not get so excited; you will have apoplexy. You will never be able to use your hands again if they are not attended to at once.'

"In his anxiety to end my mother's sufferings, he had held the basket down with both hands, never thinking of his burned hands or the pain.

"'No matter,' he answered, as he glared around on all the people assembled; 'I do not need to write, to demolish all your hopes.' And he looked at the boys with hatred. 'I have but to serve a few papers as you have these poor creatures, and the money you have looked upon as your own goes to charity.—'Not one cent,' he said, while the veins in his forehead swelled up like cords, with the anguish he was suffering, 'shall ever go to one of you, for you were all in the secret, though all may not yet have reached the fearful state of cruelty of your ringleader. Call John,' he said, and when his faithful servant came, he gave him his orders, then said, 'Now, Doctor, get your things ready; you can torture me as soon as John returns.'

"An easy-chair, table, and the lotions and bandages ordered by Doctor L. were brought out, as the patient refused to move from the spot till his work was completed.

"Soon John appeared with a small iron box in his arms, taken from the safe. His master's eyes brightened when he saw him, for he was suffering great pain.

"'Now, John, take my keys from my pocket and open that box. Jane,' he said, addressing his sister, who stood by his side, anxiety for him expressed in her face, 'take from that box the package marked "My last will and testament." Now, John, clear a space, then burn every inch of that paper in the presence of these murderers and their abettors; for it is a cruel murder, and Tige shall be avenged.'

"It was done, and no one dared interfere, though some of them knew they were seeing the hopes of years fade away and perish in that heap of ashes.

"'Now,' he said to the doctor, 'dress my burns. I am satisfied.' Just then I mewed, and he exclaimed, 'Poor little orphan! Take him out of my pocket, Jane; he shall have such tender care that this dreadful scene may be forgotten.'

"The sister took me out of his pocket very tenderly, and I clung to her, while she stood by her brother and tried to help him bear the suffering caused by the dressing of his wounds. The pain was fearful, but he said it was a pleasure to bear it, knowing that he had spared poor Tige and her kittens by ending their suffering at once.

"When the basket was taken out, my poor mother was found, her fur singed off, while one side of her was completely roasted. My little brothers and sister were just singed, for their mother had tried

65

to cover them with her body. The water had ended their lives at once. I did not see them, but I heard the people describe the horrible sight.

"By his master's orders John carried them home and buried them, after putting them in a nice box on the grounds. I will show you their grave some day before you leave.

"The uncle never forgave them. He allowed his nephew and his wife the use of the house and an annuity for life; but not one cent of his money could be used for the children.

"Their own means being small, they were obliged to give up the thought of a profession for their sons and put them into business. The uncle said very justly that no one ought to be a doctor who had no love in his heart for the dumb creatures so dependent on him for their welfare.

"He lived but two years after this, and he made me his special care. Nothing was too good for me, and I loved him with all my heart, and I know I was a great comfort to him. When I would lick the scars on his hands, I have seen the tears in his eyes, and he would smooth my fur, and say, 'Poor Tige! poor Tige!'

"He never quite recovered the use of his left hand, but he never complained; and when I was big enough I would walk out with him every day, for I distrusted every one, and made very few friends. He named me Pedro for a friend of his, a Spanish gentleman from whom he inherited some of his wealth.

"At his death he gave me to his sister, and left a large sum to be used for my benefit. He had given her a fine property and the estate where we now live. After her death it is to be used for charity and a home for animals.

"She has been very kind to me. The friends whom she has taken to live here and keep the home for her are very nice, and they understand just how I am situated. They are fond of animals, and make a great deal of me; but I can never care for people again. My mistress is not very strong, probably will not live much longer, and I hope when she dies I shall soon follow her. The horrible scene of my mother's death has taken all the pleasure of life from me. Do you wonder I do not make new friends or trust people?"

I assured him of my sympathy, saying that I hoped there were no such wicked people about now.

"Don't think that," he said; "there are hundreds of just such wicked, cruel acts committed all the time. Something should be done to stop the work now, and save the children from being murderers and criminals."

I was very unhappy over Pedro's story. I did wish my mistress could hear this sad tale, for I know that she would try to help the poor abused creatures.

I had quite an ill turn from worry of mind over this sad story, and from the internal injury that I received from the encounter with that bulldog.

My mistress was quite anxious about me. She gave me catmint tea and made me a lovely little blanket, and this with a thick shawl folded under it was placed on the lounge for my bed. I was very comfortable, and I hope a grateful cat, when I contrasted my lot with others. I did not feel (even to the dog that attacked me) any bitterness, for had he been taught better by his master, he would not have treated me like an enemy.

How can we expect a life-long prejudice, such as dogs and cats have for each other, to be uprooted, unless they are taught better by their owners and by the good examples that ought to be set before them? How can human beings boast of being better than animals?

Think of the heathen cannibals, eating human flesh. To them the fat little baby is just like a chicken. Then the Indians—did a cat ever worry a rat worse than they tortured the white men? When you think of this, can you conscientiously say we are worse, or even as bad as human beings?

There is money, and eloquence, and sympathy for the heathen; but the poor animals are left to learn without teachers what ought to be taught them, to make them the faithful servants and intelligent companions of man.

I trust the day will come when these humble friends will be as much thought of in the family as the children; there is no doubt they will fully repay all kindness done them.

XIX

MEWS AND PURRS

IN my humble opinion no one ever told stories to equal those of my friends. Miss Eleanor could tell the cutest little fox and pig stories, while Miss Milly excelled on cat stories.

During my sickness they entertained me finely. Miss Eleanor used to tell a story of the "Pig Family," and the boys were wild over it. No matter how many new ones were told, they never were satisfied to go to sleep without hearing the well-worn pig story.

One night when Miss Eleanor was away, Miss Milly put the children to bed, and of course told them stories. They were not satisfied without the pig story. She was in a hurry, and preferred to tell stories out of her own head, saying she did not know the Pig Family; that was Aunt Eleanor's story.

At last, as they would not go to sleep without it, she told it to them as she remembered it. When it was finished, she looked at Willie, and saw that his lip was quivering and his eyes were full of tears.

"What is the matter?" she said.

"You haven't told about the little blue pig," he sobbed.

"Oh, nonsense!" she said; "he is dead probably."

This finished him. He cried as if his heart would break. She said she never killed a pig before, and had such a hard time bringing that blue one to life, she never would kill another.

Now I am just like the children. I love to hear the same stories over and over, and feel really acquainted with the little creatures that they tell about. And I take after my mistress. I build "castles in the air," though I have heard her say she always got an axe ready to demolish them, for she knew they would have to go. I wish I did know what an axe is. I would have one too.

One day there was a real big snowstorm. I looked out of the window, and when I saw the big white snowflakes coming down, I did wonder about them. Miss Eleanor read one day of a little girl who, on seeing the snowflakes, asked her mother if the angels were shaking their feather beds.

What a little silly she was, for I know better than that. I do not believe even an angel would throw away feathers. They are so nice, I do love to sleep on them. But then cats know more; only they keep it to themselves.

We had a good fire in the grate, and it crackled and spluttered, and looked, as Miss Eleanor said, very homelike. Just then a young lady called at the door to return a book my mistress had loaned her. They asked her to come in and have tea with them.

She had a room in the upper story, and they had frequently invited her in to warm her, for she had no fire, and they feared she was not very well off, and they tried to befriend her without hurting her pride.

She was very pretty and well educated, and I liked her very much. She petted me and told me stories of cats she had known in her home before her father and mother had died, for she was an orphan.

She was very sad, and Miss Milly took out all her pictures and treasures to amuse her. At last she said: "I will tell you about the first cat I ever remember. He belonged to my father, and his name was Tom."

I pricked up my ears, for I was wild to hear the story of Tom. All the little anecdotes I had heard of him pleased me very much.

I think my mistress's father and mother were lovely people, and when any one comes in and speaks of having known them, I listen with all my heart. And now I was to hear all about Tom. So I got up on Miss Milly's lap, ready to devour every word.

My mistress said she did not know where Tom was born. He first made his début in one of the good old-fashioned houses now standing in Salem, of witchcraft fame. She said:—

"My father petted him with his children, and he was the ruling spirit of the house. Though not a handsome cat, he could be very fascinating. He was so coy of his marks of favor that one valued them more for their rarity. That he had blue blood in his veins no one could doubt, from the supreme contempt he evinced toward poor alley cats. He always perched himself on the highest place on the fence and looked down upon them. They looked up to him in the most abject manner, for they knew he was generous and had the right to give the contents of the swill house to them, if he pleased."

He was very fond of Miss Milly, and as she was the youngest, and not very strong, he made it his special duty to amuse her.

After having stolen a squab that had been cooked for her, and persuaded her to pretend she had eaten it, he ever after was a devoted friend to her. When they had company, Tom was a study. He inspected them with a critical eye. If satisfied, he allowed himself to be petted by them. Often, however, he would reject the offered attention, with a hiss of scorn, and make himself scarce while they remained. Their father said Tom was a good judge of character, for he turned a "cold shoulder" where he himself would have been pleased to do the same.

They had an old bachelor cousin, and their mother was his favorite aunt. The son of her eldest brother, naturally he was a welcome guest with all the family. Having no brothers of their own, they were inclined to receive Cousin Robert's oddities with favor. He would come in of an evening, and if not noticed by them would remove his wraps and soon make himself at home.

One evening, to his sorrow, Cousin Robert made them a visit. After a short conversation with his aunt, he drew near the table where his cousins were playing games. One or two smothered sounds proved his enjoyment.

Cousin Robert was rather fond of cats, but his advances to acquaintance with Tom had met with poor success. His gentle "Pussy, Pussy" and extended hand had been met with disdain. Their father said he thought that Tom resented the "Pussy" as too weak a name for his majesty.

He never approached his would-be friend and cousin or accepted his flag of truce. Their father, later on, did remember that Tom had cast unfriendly glances at Cousin Robert from his corner where he could overlook all their movements. Subsequent events explained their meaning in a manner most unfavorable to their object.

This evening the children were full of fun. The game was very attractive, and Cousin Robert never thought of Tom.

Suddenly their mother exclaimed, "What a strong smell of medicine!" Then remembering that Cousin Robert had rheumatism, and very likely it was liniment he had used, she tried to pass it over. Too late, however, for they were all sensible of a very strong medicinal smell by this time.

A low laugh from their father, who was seated in his armchair by the fire, called our attention to Tom. He was in his usual corner, engaged in a furious battle with some dark object. Just as they asked, "Is it a mouse," one fierce tug dislodged the cork from a bottle from which he had just torn the paper, and they all cried out "Valerian!"

Tom bounded out of his corner, crushing in his grasp the dark object he had battled with, and drunk with the valerian, he turned over and over in perfect abandonment.

Cousin Robert gazed with dazed eyes upon the scene; then he rushed forward, saying, "Good Godfrey! it's my—my hat!"

The shouts of laughter and the fiendish leer of Tom's eye, as he gazed upon him, rendered their poor cousin speechless, after having aired his only approach to profanity.

After a time he made grab after grab at his poor old hat. In vain, however; for Tom turned over and over, crushing it out of shape, flourishing such formidable claws every time he tried to rescue it, serving friend and foe alike, when the children tried to help their cousin, that they were obliged to give up the attempt.

Tom held the fort, and knew how to keep it; and the children were too well aware of Tom's power as an illustrator to desire to represent etchings, even by their "own artist, taken on the spot."

When at last the bottle was taken from him, only one-half of the valerian was left.

As soon as their father could command his voice, he said, "I will make good the loss of the hat, and keep Tom on short rations to pay for it."

The children were bursting with suppressed laughter at the sight of Cousin Robert, in one of their father's old hats. When they said good night to him, Tom got up, and, walking around him, cocked up his eye as if to say, "How funny you do look!"

Tom went in for his full share of the fun, when they all drew near the fire, laughing over the funny features of the scene. If his tongue was silent, his eyes were eloquent with a language they all understood.

After a time he went to his corner and returned with the poor old hat, which he laid with great dignity at his master's feet. "That settles the question," he seemed to say.

It did settle it with Cousin Robert. Though he got a new hat, it was months before he visited them again, and then Tom was put out of the room—an indignity he resented by stealing a neighbor's chicken.

It was pure wickedness, for he did not care for it himself, but gave it to the poor alley cats to devour; for he patronized them and had many disreputable pensioners. All his master said, when told of Tom's wickedness, was, "Pay for it." And to Tom he would say, "If you go on this way, you bad boy, we shall end our days in the poorhouse."

Tom looked as if he did not care where we ended our days, if we took him with us. And he was very sure his master would never go without him.

Tom carried the old felt hat up into his den in the attic, and when any unusual noise was heard, his master would say, "Tom is rehearsing his play of 'Valerian, or The Old Felt Hat.'"

I thought the story of Cousin Robert very nice, and when I lie on the lounge, looking in the fire, I can see all these scenes, and I do enjoy it. Miss Eleanor says she thinks I have a great deal of imagination. I suppose it is something nice, so I guess I have. I don't feel a bit jealous, for Miss Milly was a child then, and Tom was not her special pet, as I am; for I know that I am the "very apple of her eye," as I have heard people say, and it sounds big because I don't know what it means.

Miss Milly said she would tell more about Tom some day, for the young lady was very much pleased with his story. She looked warm and happy, and drank lots of tea, and ate crackers and had a good time generally.

Some time after, a friend called who had known them from childhood and knew Tom. Such nice reminiscences I never heard before. When she noticed me, she began talking about cats, and I thought she would never stop.

They invited her to take tea, though they laughingly said, "We have no two dishes alike, and very humble fare."

She enjoyed it, however, though she had a lovely home, servants and carriages at her command. This little bit of Bohemianism, as they called it, was a delight to her. She made them promise to spend the day with her, saying, "You can bring Daisy, for I will send a carriage for you, and my Priggy will be delighted with him."

I was pleased with the invitation, but took a dislike to Priggy at once. Such a name! Just think of it! To be called Priggy, when there are beautiful flowers and places that cats can be named for. To call a poor creature Priggy was weakness personified. I was disgusted, and refused to believe in Priggy.

As we never went to see him, my mistress not being well enough to visit, I never had the chance to express my indignation to him. Perhaps it is just as well. Poor little fool! He may think Priggy is a lovely name.

Some time after, when it stormed very hard, and the young lady upstairs was cold and low-spirited, my mistress invited her down and entertained us with more of Tom's history.

She said Tom was very fastidious in regard to dress. He despised anything ragged, and a dirty swill man (waste merchants they are called now) aroused his deepest anger. Beggars of all ages and sex he ignored. The children's dresses he looked over with a critical eye, and if he detected a rag, he would make mending impossible.

What he would have done in these days of sewing machines cannot be imagined, for he was frantic over a thread of cotton or silk, and only a knot kept the whole work from being torn to pieces by his sharp teeth.

They had one of the best-natured Pats to do their outdoor work that could be found. Pat Ryan was a faithful soul. His one great fault was his love of the bottle.

He very soon gave up the attempt of making friends with Tom, for he answered all his advances with hisses and growls, loud and deep. His tail would swell up, and he would bristle all over when Pat tried to pet him; just as human beings do when they are presumed upon by those they think beneath them in the social scale.

70

Pat had truly to earn his living by "the sweat of his brow." No modern helps for him. His whole stock in trade consisted of two large firkins on a rough wheel-barrow, to transport the waste that he went from house to house collecting.

He would have thought the millennium had come could he have looked forward to the progress of to-day,—the strong blue carts, with their well-fed high-steppers, and the Patricks of the period, seated with pipes in their mouths, and leather lap-robes, in imitation of their employers, going their rounds, pounding back gates, and bullying the servants if they were not prompt to greet them.

This improvement in the swill business might have made Pat give up his bottle and take to the nearly as demoralizing vice of smoking all the time. But his heavy wheel-barrow had no horse but himself, and the overflowing firkins were a load for him, particularly when, as was often the case, he was as full as his firkins.

It was then that Tom saw his opportunity. When Pat's gait was unsteady, his vision oblique, when he magnified his load by double firkins, double barrow, double people, and double street, Tom would swoop down upon him, and by some dexterous movement, known only to himself, cross Pat's path and overthrow his load. Then, reaching the highest place on the fence, he would look down, as if to say: "Well, you have come to grief. How did you do it?"

Pat was not deceived. Drunk or sober, he recognized his enemy, and gave him the full measure of his wrath. "Ye limb of Satan," he would say, "ye'll get it yet!" Such promises were never realized. Old Cloven-foot only could compete with this clever cat.

One unlucky day Pat came earlier than usual, and finding the gate closed, had to reach his arm over to unfasten it. It was quite a stretch over the top of the fence, and Pat's head did not come even with the top, so that he could not look over.

Tom, who was looking on, at once took in the situation. He crawled on his belly on the ledge of the fence just below the top, and every time Pat would reach over his hand, Tom would grab it with his open paws, his claws as sharp as needles.

Yelling with rage and pain, realizing that it was his enemy, Tom, poor Pat, unwilling to give up, tried and tried again, only to be served in the same manner.

At last he mounted on the barrow, bringing his head on a level with the fence. Before he could gain advantage from this move Tom had grabbed with both paws Pat's old straw hat, rushing like mad up to the house.

Pat had by this time forced an entrance, and ran after him, in pursuit of his old hat, calling on all the saints to demolish Tom. Bareheaded, with torn and bleeding hands, witnesses of his wrongs, Pat poured forth his tale of woe to his friends in the kitchen, where he found sympathy, for Tom was feared by all the servants. Of course the culprit was nowhere to be seen.

Their mistress soon healed the breach, if not the wound, by giving Pat an old hat. To be sure, it was rather too respectable looking for his calling, but then, he was satisfied even if it did not accord with the rest of his outfit. No salve for his wound would have equalled that hat.

Miss Milly said as she watched him from her window, walking off with his new hat on, Tom crawled out from under the sofa, and, mounting the arm of her chair, said in cat language, "Don't he look just like Cousin Robert?"

Miss Milly said that when her father came home, Tom ran to meet him; then he took his master's slippers, and carried them to his chair.

71

"What means this unusual demonstration?" asked his master. Tom hung his head and walked under the chair. Then, when his master was seated, he crawled out, and, mounting to the arm of his chair, rubbed against his shoulder. Secure of his position, he looked around on them, as if to say, "Now tell all you know." With his large eyes fixed on their faces, he enjoyed over again his adventures, wagging his tail in recognition of the telling points in the story they related to their father.

His master said: "Tom's ancestors must have been in the hat trade, he is so fond of hats. We shall have to establish a branch of the business, and make Tom the head. If he goes on in this way, we cannot find hats enough to pay his debts."

Tom enjoyed it, looking at Miss Milly as if to say, "Don't I do it to keep up her spirits?"

He did not come in contact with Pat for some time, for Pat prudently kept out of his way. His cunning only slumbered, however. They called it turning over a new leaf; but one day he came out with a new joke on Pat.

"Looking from my window," Miss Milly said, "one morning, I saw quite an army of cats assembled around the plank walk leading to the swill house. Tom, seated on the highest post in the yard, surveyed them with great satisfaction, which was shown by the proud elevation of his head.

"His most gracious manner was explained when Pat, coming in, dispersed them, and a long array of bones was exposed to view—the remains of the feast Tom had invited them to partake of.

"Pat could not do justice to the subject. Shaking his fist at Tom, who never winked, but gazed with solemn eyes at him, he said: 'Ye mane crathur, ye are a human for spite, picking out the best for the old alley cats ye hates. I will get a dog.' Tom only yawned, and said as plain as cat could say, 'How tiresome!' After he had watched poor Pat picking up the leavings, muttering all the time hatred of his enemy, he came to me for approval. My mother being in the room, she put him in the attic, telling him he ought to be punished by solitary confinement.

"He soon procured his release by making such a racket over my head, running about, upsetting marbles, then chasing them about, that I was very glad to open the door and say, 'You bad cat, come down.' He came when he got ready, very slowly, and was quite cool to me, though I told him he had made my head ache with his racket.

"He was not a neighborly cat, never visiting, as cats often do, the neighbors' houses, and he treated their cats with the greatest disdain. He often fed them. I have seen him pick open the waste-house door, claw out a lot of bread and bones for the benefit of the hungry crowd. Then he would mount the fence and look on. 'With them, but not of them,' was his motto.

"Though he did not visit around, he knew everything going on in the street. He overlooked the butcher, baker, and grocer, and knew every grain of provision carried into the houses, even going so far as smelling of the meat; but when offered anything, he refused with such contempt that one and all came to look upon him as a very aristocratic cat.

"Every carriage that came to the street was received by him. He always waited till the trunks were carried in, the driver paid, and then he would come home satisfied.

"A friend of ours, who boarded in the next house, had just returned from her country home. Tom, being a favorite of hers, received her, and superintended the removal of her trunks with great interest. He followed her into the house and remained some time. When my mother called him home, he came very unwillingly.

"The next morning after breakfast he disappeared. This was nothing unusual, as my father said, 'Probably Tom had some business needing his attention daily.'

"In the afternoon, when my mother called on our friend, she found Tom had dined there.

"After a time, this lady, remembering that she had brought me a book from her home, proposed going up to her trunk for it. Shortly after, she called my mother, who, with the lady of the house, went up to the attic where the trunks were kept. There they found Tom with two of the house cats seated on a huge trunk that had not been opened. The trunk bore marks of their claws, as scratches long and deep had torn and disfigured the leather.

"The scene was most laughable. Tom looked wise (nothing could embarrass him), while the others looked sheepish. They could not be induced to leave their perch, and at last light dawned on the situation, when the friend said, 'Do you think Tom remembers that I promised him some fresh catmint from the country?' 'Undoubtedly,' said my mother; 'he not only remembers, but he smells it.'

"The catmint was soon produced, and they all had a feast. Tom wanted to stay and have a free fight after he had eaten his fill; but my mother let him see the large bag she carried home, and he followed her unwillingly. He knew where it was kept, and would go and mew before the closet door till he got his catmint. After it was gone, on seeing the empty bag, he went over to our friend's, and up to the trunk. Nothing would satisfy him but looking in and seeing it was empty.

"For some time he was cool to our friend, but after a few days, remembering perhaps that she might go home and get him more, he accepted her marks of affection with quiet dignity.

"Tom was very thoughtful. When told not to do certain things, he was very ready to obey. His master would say, 'Tom, did I not tell you never to get into my chair unless there is a covering on it?' and Tom would look as ashamed while the hairs were brushed off, and would avoid the chair for a long time, and once he was seen to pull the tidy down from the back, and sit on it. As it was lace, and he tore a hole in it, his thoughtfulness was appreciated only by his master.

"Tom was not a cat for every one to love. He had very little reverence in his composition. My father and mother," Miss Milly continued, "were very hospitable, and always at the church gatherings entertained all they could accommodate. Unlike the children of to-day, we were kept in the background.

"One of our guests was an old travelling preacher—'colporteur,' as he was called, since he carried about religious books for sale. There is no doubt he sold many, for buying a book was a more simple thing than arguing with him, his tongue being one of the most aggressive.

"Every morning the family were early called to prayers, kneeling down before chairs in the long room, having to remain in that position while this old man prayed for every one around, calling them by name. All fared alike. Though I do not believe he remembered our faces, he never forgot our names. My name, unfortunately, was taken from Shakespeare, and not from some heroine of religious fiction; and I suffered more when mine was called than my sister did, nearly all of the family having good Bible names that he enjoyed repeating. It is not necessary to say how long he lingered over it to impress its worldliness on his listeners. It was to me like opening a wound every morning.

"Tom, however, paid him for it. Perhaps he did not like his own name being left out. An additional cause for revenge, no doubt, was that when once he passed the reverend gentleman, the humane Christian put out his foot, giving Tom a slight kick, and said, 'What a great beast!' This was enough to arouse Tom's ire, even if not mentioning him with the family had not been enough. So one morning Tom attended family prayers.

"Now this old man wore shoes tied with good strong strings, with little tags on the ends. Tom looked at them and saw his opportunity. Just in the middle of the prayer he pounced upon one of the long strings, giving a pull with his sharp, strong teeth that made the words in the mouth of his victim come out with a jerk.

"Of course Tom fled at the sound, and after a time the prayer continued. Finally, just as we were hoping for the last clause, it came in the shape of Tom, who rushed out from under the sofa, and with one wrench untied the other shoe, while the amen came out with a bound. Then we had to listen to a long harangue on the sin of keeping animal pets where we could feed poor children.

"My father and mother listened respectfully, but made no promise of turning God's dumb creatures out to starve. My elder sister quoted to us:—

"'He prayeth best who loveth bestAll things, both great and small;For the dear God that loveth us,He made and loveth all.'

But then, the 'Ancient Mariner' himself could not have convinced this ancient bigot.

"Tom kept out of the way for some time, but we did not trust him. After untying his enemy's shoes, we were afraid he would attack his brown wig. My mother every morning made sure he was out of the way before we went to prayers.

"How it happened, we never knew, but Tom outwitted her, and one morning, the last of the visitor's stay at our house, Tom made his mark, gaining a place in our memory never to be filled by any other cat.

"Just at the close of a long prayer Tom crept along stealthily toward the chair of his enemy. No one was in a position to see him; but when he crawled by the lounge where I was lying, I felt his presence, and my heart seemed to stand still, for I knew he was bent on mischief. I dared not move, and had to watch him with bated breath as he gained on his unconscious prey. Now his noble enemy never bowed his head in prayer, but, kneeling before a chair, his hands spread out, his eyes closed, his body swaying to and fro, presented a very undignified appearance.

"No doubt Tom thought so, for he walked around and faced him, looking in his face through the opening in the back of the chair for a long time. Suddenly he made a grab (I think he intended to catch the fluttering end of the necktie), but just then the preacher lowered his head, and Tom's claws came down full on the bridge of his nose with such force that the words of the prayer were shouted in a manner suggesting profanity.

"All was confusion, as the enraged old man started to his feet, prayer and religion alike forgotten in his desire for revenge. Too late, however; for Tom rushed from the room, his tail up in the air, like a flag of victory. He did not appear again until all trace of our visitor was removed.

"Poor old man! He did look abject, with the blood dripping over the end of his nose, and tears of rage and pain in his eyes. Never did piety disappear so quickly as it did from this good old man, in view of his wrongs. One would have thought Tom possessed of human intelligence to hear him denounced. My sister said she believed he was sorry that Tom had no soul to be lost, thus to appease his wrath.

"My mother produced salve and some court-plaster and made him as comfortable as possible, but without receiving any thanks. He left us, very indignant that my father would not promise to have Tom killed. He refused to remain to breakfast, saying he would not take another meal in the house with that 'ungodly cat.'

"As my father paid all his expenses, and my mother gave him new and warm clothing, he had no reason to be offended. My sister said he was a 'wolf in sheep's clothing,' and Tom knew it, and had been trying to protect us against him.

"Tom spent the night at a neighbor's, coming home the next day in a most amiable frame of mind and a very (for him) humble air. Instead of running to meet my father as usual, he kept in his corner, pretending to be asleep. No one spoke to him, and he bore it as long as he could; then he walked over to my father, and, putting a paw on each knee, looked up in his face with a piteous mew.

"Poor father could not bear that. His tender heart was touched, and he put his hand on Tom's head, saying, 'Oh, Tom, I am so sorry you are such a wicked boy!' but the tone assured Tom, who at once jumped up on my father's shoulder and kissed his face with delight.

"All through the long sermon preached to him of his sins he sat very quiet, and never once winked, but kept his wide-open, wise eyes on his master; at last he yawned two or three times, and then washed his face. But peace was established.

"'What a character that man will give you, Tom, wherever he goes,' said my mother.

"Tom shook his head as if to say: 'Such is fame. I always wanted to be famous. Then, I love to etch, particularly on noses, and that was a good big one. I enjoyed it.'

"Poor Tom! I can hardly tell of his death even now, after so many years, without the swelling in my throat, to keep back the tears caused by deep sorrow for my pet.

"One night he went out and did not return till morning. The door of one of the outbuildings was left open for him to go in if he pleased, but he never came home till morning; then, as we learned from the servants, he went up to his den in the attic. At noon time he did not come down, and my sister went in search of him and found him dead.

"He was not in his nice little basket bed, of which he was very proud; but lay on some old relics, among the most noticeable of which was the old hat of Cousin Robert.

"He had been poisoned. His bright face was all green, and his brilliant eyes were glassy. We could not even rub and kiss his dear old nose as he liked us to, for drops had run down from his mouth and stained the beautiful fur coat we loved so well, and my mother said we must not touch him.

"Under the pile of things where he lay was an open map of the United States; he had trampled it down some time before. We often said he studied it when alone. Tom was closed up in this map, with a large rug outside, and buried in the river.

"How we mourned for him and how changed was that lovely river view to me! I could never have been consoled, had not a dear old lady said to me,—

"'Why do you mourn so for your precious pet?'

"'Ah,' I said, 'I shall never, never see him again.'

"'Why not?' she asked.

"'Because cats have no souls, no after life.'

"'My child,' she answered, 'God never gave us these dear, affectionate creatures to care for and then part with forever. You will have your dear Tom again where perfect happiness is secured by just such meetings.'

"I think she was right; and as good Dr. Watts so beautifully describes in that well-known Baptist hymn, 'Sweet Fields beyond the Swelling Flood,' there is no doubt there we shall find our faithful dumb friends.

"My father never recovered from Tom's loss. He would not take his accustomed place by the fire where Tom had been his companion for so many years, and he never made a pet of any of the many cats we had, though they were very bright ones.

"My dear good father! I have very little recollection of him, as he died while I was quite young. But I never remember him without Tom seated in all his glory by his side."

When Miss Milly had finished her story we were all subdued by the death of Tom; but then he had a happy life, so I just winked off my tears and hoped I should know him in heaven.

XX
HEADS AND TALES

I DID not recover my cheerfulness after hearing the story of Tom, and Miss Eleanor said she hoped Miss Milly would never repeat it again.

The young lady friend had wiped her eyes often, and I was very glad when they made her some hot ginger tea and packed her off to her room. They said she had a cold in her head, but I know better. It was Tom and his death that had gone to her head and made her eyes water. It was what made me cough and sneeze and wink, to keep from the womanish weakness of tears.

Good gracious! I shall have hysterics next, if I have got to hear such doleful things. I am ashamed of myself. I thought I had more dignity. Pshaw! I was not crying. It is that horrid musk that I smell; it always makes my eyes water. I am glad my mistress never uses it, and I do wish, if people come here to be warmed and comforted and entertained, they would not wear perfume. I do despise it. I shall have to chew a lot of catmint and roll in it before I feel like myself again.

I know that when I went to Beverly I rode over that very river where Tom was buried. I am very glad I did not know it then, and I am very glad that some day I shall see all these dear people. Of course I know just how indignant some will be to read this. I think it very strange that there are so many who do not want any one to go to heaven but those they approve. They scorn the idea that God should save the creatures he has made, because they call them a lower order of beings.

I have said more than I ought to on this subject, for my mistress always says when any one begins upon it, "We will not discuss it, if you please, for we shall not agree." And I always like to please her and do as she says; and then, I do lose my temper and have such bad feelings that I fear I shall be counted with the bad ones, whom Dante says are shadows in the other world. And of all things I think a shadow is a "little too thin." I am glad my mistress cannot hear this, for she hates slang.

Some days ago a lady was here, and she started that endless subject of "servants." My mistress tried to turn the conversation, but it was of no use. The servant question, when one gets on it, is like a brook; it goes on forever. To be sure, I did hear a young man once say something that would stop it, and my mistress hushed him up at once; but not before I had heard it, and it sounded so forcible that I went under the bed and said it, and wondered if it would stop the women from talking about their servants. They did not say it often, as my mistress did not know I had heard it.

Always after the people who discussed their servants had gone, Miss Eleanor would say, "Now I will read something to take away the disagreeable impression."

It was usually Dickens, for he seems to have got at the very heart of things, and his poor are shown up with hearts, while the higher classes are heartless oftentimes.

76

Of course this is only given you second-hand, but I comprehend it, else I should not repeat it.

I do dote on Dickens, and I think "David Copperfield" is my special favorite. Aunt Betsey Trotwood seems like a real aunt to me. Dear little Dora! I was very wretched when she died, and I loved Jip. I know he would have played with me very nicely.

When Miss Eleanor read about his death, there was a lump in her throat, and Miss Milly's eyes were full of tears, and I thought it was time for me to go under the bed, not for any particular reason, only there are times when one likes to be alone.

While I am writing I would like, if possible, to correct any bad impression regarding cats and their habits. It has been said that cats will draw the breath of an infant and sometimes of older people while sleeping. I deny this, and will tell you a story which illustrates the superstition, and was told by one of our friends.

This lady visited us one day, and while talking about me and cats in general, she said she had always thought cats were not to be trusted, and never allowed her children to play with one, for the very foolish beliefs of which I have spoken. "But," she said, "I have changed my opinion, and now think a cat properly trained is a noble creature." Then she told us this story:—

"You remember my cousin, of course, for I know you probably have visited at my uncle's. They were very fond of cats, always keeping two or three. When my cousin was married, she took with her one of her old cat's kittens. She was quite well grown, and was called Dido. She was a great pet with my cousin's husband, and as it was his first experience of cats, he was delighted with her playfulness.

"They were fortunate in having servants who were kind to cats. Just after the first child was born one of the husband's relatives died, leaving him a large old country place—a farmhouse with a great many acres of land. He was very much pleased, for he said the country air would be good for baby and its mother, for she was very delicate since the birth of her beautiful boy.

"The house had not been occupied for some time, and was one of those old, rambling, picturesque places, a delight to lovers of the olden times. The furniture was substantial, but very severe in style.

"'You need not take the boy's bassinet,' said the father, laughing; 'for there was a cradle that looked as if it had come from Noah's Ark, and Shem, Ham, and Japhet, not to speak of all the two-by-twos, had been rocked in it.'

"'Oh,' said his wife, 'how lovely that will be! we can fill it with pillows, and baby will be delighted with it.'

"'Nonsense,' said her husband; 'don't go and build "castles in the air" out of that old cradle. It will do for Dido to sleep in; but on the whole, you had better take the bassinet and all the other folderols for Baby, else you will be homesick.'

"She decided, however, that she would take nothing with her, but enjoy all the old-fashioned surroundings.

"The place proved very satisfactory, and she found a nice large room leading out of hers for the baby's nursery.

"The large pointed-top mahogany cradle was duly polished and installed in the room, making a royal bed for his highness the baby. With its wealth of pillows and lace coverings it looked quite regal.

"The nurse girl was very devoted to Baby, always watching him while he slept. Dido had appropriated the baby ever since his birth, and would allow his little soft hand to take liberties with her, pulling her tail, when she would resent it in others. She spent much of her time in the house, watching the baby.

"About a week after they had settled comfortably at home they were called up from the piazza by the screams of the husband's sister, who was visiting them. All she could say was, 'That cat—that cat—has killed the baby!'

"They rushed into the room, and a strange sight met their eyes. Standing in the cradle, with a paw each side of the baby, was Dido.

"The poor mother rushed to the cradle, crying, 'Oh, my baby, my baby!'

"Her husband drew her back, saying, 'Look there.' At the side of the cradle were two great rats that Dido had killed just as they were about to attack the baby.

"Dido was bleeding from a wound in the neck, where they had bitten her, but she kept her watch over the baby till her friends arrived. She mewed out her thanks when they petted her and praised her. The baby had slept through it all.

"The aunt said she was just coming out of her room when she heard Dido give a shrill cat call, and she went in, but seeing her over the baby, supposed she had drawn its breath and killed it.

"They were so grateful to Dido that they would not rest till the doctor had been sent for to dress her wounds. They soon healed, and after this Dido seemed to have the care of the baby on her mind; and the cradle being long, a rug was put in at the foot, and after the matting was put over the top Dido would lie on it to keep it down. That she slept with one eye open, they were sure; for if the baby opened his eyes, Dido would either mew or go for them.

"They found the large closet in the room full of rat holes, and as the room had been unused for so long, they infested it.

"They removed to a smaller room, and as they took precautions, were soon free from rats. Probably the latter knew they had a powerful enemy in Dido, and left.

"There were three cats belonging to the house that had left when it was closed; but on finding it inhabited again, they had returned, as cats love to keep to one home. They were well treated, and repaid the kindness by clearing the house of rats.

"As the family left the man and his wife who had worked for them in the house during the winter, they never had trouble with rats again.

"They had a picture of Dido taken with the baby, and all their friends made a great fuss over her."

I did wish I could see this picture; for Miss Milly always shows me pictures, and I enjoy them very much. Why, I could take the photograph cases and tell you every one, if I could speak.

Sometimes we have real fun over the old-fashioned ones. My mistress laughs with us, and says, "This is the family 'Rogues' Gallery,' they do look so funny." And they never show them to strangers, for they say we love them too well to let any one else laugh at their old-fashioned looks.

I do love pictures, but I have been taken to places where they had horrid crayons on the walls, and the eyes stared at me so I did want to scratch them out. I hate a chromo, but a nice, peaceful landscape makes me happy; and I often see one where I would like to lie down and dream, for a cat can have real artistic taste.

I don't think I care much for babies. I suppose it is because I have never been around them; and when I have been, the mothers have never allowed me to get acquainted with them.

I was very cross one day when a friend of my mistress brought her baby to see us. It was all dressed in white, with a white astrachan hood with goats' hair fringe, and it looked just like a little poodle. I wanted to lick it all over when Miss Milly said, "Here, Daisy; come and see this dear baby." But its mother cried out, "Oh, don't let that horrid cat touch my baby!" just as if I was a bear or a tiger.

I was so insulted I just walked into a corner. But the baby had seen me, and held out its little hand and crowed. I looked away, but my mistress said, "Daisy will not hurt your baby," and she took me in her arms and let the baby put his soft little hand on my ear. It laughed and crowed, while I licked its hand. The mother looked as if she thought I would devour it.

When Miss Milly put me down, seeing the mother's uneasiness, the way that innocent little creature yelled, kicked, and beat his mother was dreadful. I fled under the bed, saying to myself, "How glad I am that we are unmarried people, with no children to raise a tempest for nothing."

The mother excused him by saying, "He was excited seeing that great cat." I thought, "And the great cat was excited seeing and hearing the Old Adam in that child."

I know my mistress was glad to get rid of them, and Miss Eleanor, who is very fond of children, said, "How beautiful that child would have been had it not been for its mother's foolishness."

Before I get too stupid or too old, I must tell you a delightful story of one of the witch cats of old Salem and her little mistress, sweet Hope Farley, a little lame girl my mistress knew and loved.

After I have had my "forty winks" and my nerves forget that baby, I shall remember it all.

XXI

JETT

THE story I am about to tell you has for its chief interest a little lame girl, very sweet and lovely, who died in old Salem many years ago. I think good children are almost as nice as good little kittens.

As Jett belonged to this little girl, I must tell you about her, that you may know how devotedly a cat can return affection and kindness. This is the moral of my story, and I tell it to you in the beginning, though I know morals usually come on the end. And then people have got all the interest of the story and they skip the moral. It is better that it should leaven the whole story.

Everything about Salem has a fascination for me, and I often think how nice it would be to fly through the air and take a peep at the people beneath me; but then, this pleasure is given only to black cats, and there is no use for any other colored cat to wish for it.

Little Hope Farley lived in a big, old-fashioned house, with a lovely garden around it. All the rooms were long and wide, with deep window seats, cushioned, and very comfortable—a nice place for a cat to sleep and enjoy herself.

In one of these nice roomy window seats little Hope would lie, with Jett curled up by her side. But I must not anticipate; I will tell the story just as I heard it from Miss Milly.

Hope was motherless; her father's sister had made up to her as well as any one ever can the loss of her mother. Aunt Martha was a charming woman of about forty-five, and she took little Hope into her heart at once.

(Dear me! How I wish cats had aunts! I do think they are just the nicest people to care for the unfortunate that can be found.)

Hope's father was a literary man, buried in his studies and books. When a man is that way inclined, he might, for all the good he is to his family, be buried in earnest. Then they would have his memory, and one could read on his tombstone how great a man he was, and the papers could praise him and speak of virtues that nothing but his death would ever have brought to light.

Aunt Martha was abroad when his wife died, and Hope, who was but three years old, was left to the care of a nurse.

Some carelessness caused her to fall, and a curvature of the spine and lameness for life were the consequence.

Dear me! These "curvatures" and such big words will kill me; but I must tell this story just as my mistress told it to me, for if ever she reads this little book, I want her to know how well I remember all she said.

After Hope met with the accident that crippled her for life, her father wrote to his sister to return and care for his unfortunate child and his helpless self.

She willingly accepted the charge, and soon found she had a "white elephant" on her hands. Her brother buried himself in his books, and to her care was left not only his child, but the whole household. He did pay the bills, but it was because he had the money; else he would have left even that to her, for she had a good fortune of her own.

Hope repaid her for her care by loving her with all her heart, and they were very happy together.

The beautiful garden was a great source of pleasure to them all. Even the father would walk up and down with his hands behind him; and although he did not seem to notice anything, the air, the fragrance of the flowers, and the peace of the scene probably gave him strength.

Around the sides of the garden, by the high fence, were currant bushes thick and plenty. The fruit was large, red, and tempting, and the flowers of every kind growing in their native beauty made the spot an earthly paradise. There were tall hollyhocks, double leafed, red and white, bachelors'-buttons, beds of pinks, and roses of every variety, lilies of the valley, modest but bound to be noticed for their rare fragrance, and beds of pansies that would have made the fortune of the florist. But here no thought of money crept in to mar the beauty of God's free gift, the beautiful flowers.

The garden sloped down, joining the land belonging to the next house, that faced on the side street. The low fence was broken, and just where the gate had hung, a hedge fence supplied its place, as the gate had fallen to pieces. The rank weeds and flowers grew in tangles; Nature seemed to have fought with Art, and to have gained the victory.

The estate had been unoccupied for years, the owner having just died far away from home, where he had been for years in pursuit of health. His heir, a distant cousin, was expected to make his home here; as his business was in Boston, it would be very convenient.

Great curiosity was expressed regarding the newcomers, particularly as there was a mystery regarding the neglect of the place for so many years; and a mystery in old Salem always wore a bewitching air.

About ten days after their arrival my story commences.

It was way down near the broken gate, under the sheltering boughs of an old apple tree, that a most luxurious seat had been contrived. Like a couch, it was protected at the back by cushions like the seat.

It was high noon of a sultry day in June, yet the thick leaves of the old apple tree formed a perfect shade for the dear little child reposing in this lovely retreat. The little silent figure and the crutches, leaning against the seat, told the whole melancholy tale: little Hope Farley was a cripple.

The soft hum of bees and insects filled the air, and the scent of flowers perfumed all around, and the bright blue sky above, lending its soft light, made her seem a part and portion of this charming picture of nature. Her doll, her dearest companion, was by her side. She had given her the quaint old-fashioned name of Joanna, and never suffered it to be abbreviated.

She held conversations with her, and confided all her little troubles to her wooden ear. (It would be well if wooden ears and cats' ears were the only ones to hear secrets, would it not? I must put in my cat's oar once in a while, for, you see, this story is a big one for a cat to remember.)

This day Joanna was particularly unsatisfactory, and Hope, getting tired of her airs, said:—

"Joanna, why are you so silent? Don't you hear the bees, and can't you see that great speckled toad under the currant bushes, hopping about? Oh, no, you don't like such things. You prefer flowers. Well," after a pause, "so do I. And I do love you, you dear, dear dolly." And she hugged her in her arms.

A slight crackling of the bushes and a scornful laugh caused Hope to start and look up, just as a lad of about twelve years of age presented himself on the other side of the hedge. He was a big, fair-haired boy, handsome, but rough looking, and rude as a young bear.

"What do you do that for, you little silly? That old doll don't know anything! Come, and let's play something."

Hope looked at him with wide-open eyes.

"Sulky little monkey!" he indignantly exclaimed, "why don't you speak? Say," after a pause, while he regarded her with surprise, "why don't you want to play?"

She looked at him in pathetic silence, then her eyes glanced at her crutches.

As he followed her glance, surprise, sorrow, and pity transformed his face. After a time he said in a subdued voice:—

"I am sorry I was so rude. I did not know. May I come over there?"

Hope saw how sincere he was, and in her quaint way welcomed him. He soon cleared the barrier, and seated on the stump of a tree they were very soon acquainted.

Every day after that they met, and soon became fast friends, exchanging childish confidences and mutually petting Joanna, for Jack was loyal to all of Hope's belongings.

(Now I must draw a breath, and put in my cat's oar. I have made you acquainted with Jett's two stanch friends, and you will better understand the story. I do pity Hope, for my shoulder troubles me very much, and I have to wait before I jump as I used to, and I know that she suffered, and I am very glad she had a cat to comfort her. I think sometimes if I could see these beautiful places and run around among the flowers, how happy I should be; but that is one of my air castles. But in the hereafter I know it will all be mine, and the gardens and fields of Paradise compensate for those we have not here. Now I will return to my story.)

One day, after Jack had been a long time silent, he suddenly said, "Have you got a step-mother?"

"A step-mother? What is that? My mother is an angel. She died when I was two years old."

"Well," he said, "you will have one, never fear; your father will get one. My mother died when I was five years old, and now—a year ago—my father went and got one. So will yours."

"You bad boy! He won't. My Aunt Martha won't let him. You are a dreadful boy to talk so!"

"Don't be down on a fellow so. Much you know about men. Your father's no better than mine. He'll get a wife yet, see if he don't; and you will hate her just as I do my step-mother."

"My father loved me till this woman came. He used to take me everywhere with him, and he cried when I begged for my mother after she died; he hugged me and called me his poor little chap. And now it is all over. I have never called her mother, and I never will. She killed Pipkin, my mother's cat, just as soon as she came. She made the servant drown her, because she was treacherous and broke a saucer, and she was afraid of her.

"She is a beast. Dear old Pipkin is better off away from her; but I do miss her and will never forgive that woman. My mother would kiss me, and then Pipkin and the kitty would lie beside me for company; and after my mother died that cat was all the comfort I had. The servants loved her. Not one of them would have killed her, but this woman has servants who will do her dirty work.

"She has red cheeks and a white skin, and a big mouthful of teeth that she is showing all the time, just like old Towzer, the bulldog."

"Why does she hate you?" Hope asked. "Can't you make her like you?"

"What a little goose you are! Like me? Not she. She wants me to die, to get my money that my mother left me. She told my father he ought to take board for me, for I had more money than they had. 'What,' he said, 'take board for my own son?' This did touch poor dad; but she soft-sawdered him. And then I wanted to run away, and I will some day, and join Uncle Jack, for whom I am named. He is in India. He loved my mother, his sister, and he would care for me. But you see I do love dad; and now I could not leave you."

Hope smiled such a sweet look upon him, saying, "You are a dear good boy, and my Aunt Martha will be a mother to you just as she has been to me."

And in truth this childish friendship had worked wonders in Hope. She was able to walk about the garden with her crutches and his help, for he was very careful of her, and proud to be of use in amusing her. Aunt Martha took the bright, honest boy into her heart, and he loved her dearly.

One day when Jack came over the hedge he found Hope in great excitement. Her apron covered some mystery that was very soon revealed—a coal-black cat, perfect in every way, a real witch cat, with not one mark about her from the tip of her ear to the end of her tail. Yellow eyes of the most unfathomable depth and a spasmodic wag of the tail proved her temper to be of the peppery kind.

"Where did you get her?" asked Jack.

"She came to us. When Aunt Martha opened the door this morning to take in the paper, she walked in. She came into the dining room, and when I called her, she jumped up in my lap and drank milk from a saucer. She bites and claws the rest if they touch her, but licks my hands and purrs when I talk to her. Where she came from I do not know, but I love her already almost" (with a remorseful look at Joanna) "as well as I do my dear dolly."

"I should think so," replied Jack. "I can't see how you can care so much for that old doll."

"Oh, don't, Jack! She is a dear, lovely, good old girlie" (with a hug and a kiss on Joanna's old battered face).

This Jett resented. Flying at Joanna, she stuck her sharp claws in her blond hair, dragging out a big tuft of it.

Jack shouted, "Go it! go ahead! tear her old wig off!"

Hope relieved and comforted her dear dolly, pushing the black termagant from her lap, and saying to Jack: "You are a cruel boy. I will have nothing to do with you."

This Jack could not bear, for he was a tender-hearted little fellow.

"Oh, come now," he said, "don't be so hard on a fellow. I never knew anything about dolls. I daresay Joanna is very nice. See here, perhaps I can mend her head." And he did very skilfully, and thus restored peace.

Then came the question of naming the cat.

"How would Nig do?" said Hope.

"Oh, don't! She had a dog called Nig, and it died. I was glad of it."

"Oh, no; if she had anything named Nig I will not have Kitty called so." Hope was firm in her belief in Jack's wrongs, and disliked his step-mother with all her heart. "We must call her something of that kind, for she is jet-black."

"Well," said Jack, "you have just said it. Why not call her Jett?"

So Jett she was named, to their great satisfaction.

"She must be half mine, and I will bring her all the scraps I can, for cats want no end of meat. That is," he said, "if I can get anything. She would like to starve me. She says I have such a rude appetite that it makes her sick."

"What a horrid woman! I don't believe your appetite is big; and if ever you are hungry, just let me know, and my Aunt Martha will give you all you can eat, for she loves to see me relish anything." And it was quite noticeable how often little nice things were brought out for Jack, quite accidentally, to save his pride.

"Oh, never mind," he said; "only it's a bothering shame father is so generous he never can see what is going on. We never had such meanness and scrimping before. There was always enough and to spare. Now there is not enough to feed a cat on. And a dog she will not let me have. She says that they are gluttons."

But I must curtail my story; it is getting too long.

Jack had a parrot called Bimbo. As it was a gift from his rich uncle, he was allowed to keep it.

With Joanna, Jett, and Bimbo the children were very happy. Bimbo was very happy on the bough of the old apple tree. He was deeply interested in Hope, and eyed her in a most sympathizing manner.

The first time he saw her use her crutches he gave vent to a succession of groans, and moved first one foot and then the other as if in pain, and after that he would move to a branch over her couch, and look down upon her in the most affectionate manner. Often he would astonish them by some remark drawn from the storehouse of memory.

No wonder Jett was jealous of him. When she first heard him speak, she opened wide her eyes, and stared at him in astonishment. The children shouted with laughter, and Bimbo kept up a silly cackle, encouraged by their approval. This was very provoking to Jett, as cats do not like to be laughed at, and she resented it in Bimbo.

After she had given him a scratch that he remembered he looked at her with fear and trembling. He soon learned to say "Jett." Though he said it in a soft, hesitating manner, she was deeply offended. She would give him a look that would keep him silent for hours.

She never could understand why such an uncouth-looking bird should have the power of speech given to him, while a handsome, intelligent cat could not speak at all; and the mystery of it made her very savage to poor Bimbo.

Of course the children shared their confidences with their pets, and if Mrs. Thornton had fallen into the clutches of Bimbo or Jett, she would probably have borne marks of the encounter. Joanna's wrath was suppressed; sometimes, however, silent wrath is the deepest.

One day they were in earnest conversation, Jack relating his wrongs; while Bimbo, seated on his bough, listened in silence. Suddenly, to their surprise, he said in a subdued voice: "She's an old devil! so she is! how droll! Ha! ha! ha!" ending with, "Well, I never!"

The children were convulsed with laughter. Even Aunt Martha could not resist the ludicrous situation. Bimbo, in great delight, gave a succession of "ha-ha's," ending with "Oh, she's a devil!" Aunt Martha covered him with her apron, and silence at once ensued; for he knew that was a mark of disgrace.

"Oh, Aunt Martha," said Jack, in a whisper, "don't you think it strange that Bimbo knows all about her?"

"Nonsense!" she replied. "Did you ever hear Bimbo swear before?"

"Never. He used, when I first had him, to say a few bad words, but covering him up made him know he must not repeat them; but to-day he has applied them where they are true. Whenever she is around, he swears all the time, and I keep him out of her way, for he knows her. She says I taught him. It is false. Uncle Jack bought him of some sailors. They gave him a good character, and Uncle Jack said if he ever used bad words, it would teach me a lesson never to say anything I did not want him to repeat."

"Very wise of your uncle. You must do as he has advised, and you will soon teach him better."

Just here, Jett, who had been a silent witness of the scene, could bear it no longer. She flew up the tree and out on the bough where Bimbo sat in disgrace, and drawing off the apron with sheathed claws, she boxed him right and left.

Poor Bimbo retreated to the very edge of the bough, screaming "Jett, Jett! oh, oh, Jett!" This offended her so much that Jack had to pull her down by her tail, to save Bimbo's life.

She was of course very much disgusted at such unusual treatment, and went off in the sulks. After a time peace was restored, and Bimbo was happy, for they were all very kind and sympathizing, and Hope smoothed his feathers where Jett had attacked him, and Jack told him he was forgiven provided he never swore again.

Aunt Martha told the children a nice, interesting story, while Jack held Bimbo on his arm, and Hope cuddled Joanna in her lap.

This home picture was interrupted by Bridget, the cook. She came, full of wrath, to enter her complaint of Jett, who followed in the distance as bold as a lion. Bridget said she put some squash pies she had made to cool for dinner, and she found Jett sitting in the middle of one while she was eating from the other, her paws and tail going as fast as her tongue.

Jack shrieked with laughter when he saw her glossy black fur covered with squash. Her nose and whiskers were dotted with it, and even her ears had little yellow decorations.

As soon as Aunt Martha could command her voice, she consoled Bridget by telling her she would make a dessert in place of the pies. Then she told Jett she had better go and get into the waste barrel. And a sight she was—a picture in yellow and black.

She went away, ashamed,—not, however, without casting a look of fury at Bimbo, who was whispering with a smothered chuckle, "Oh, she's a dear! she's a dear! Oh, oh, Jett! I shall die!"

Jett preferred a crooked path. Stealing was her delight, for boldly, in the face of all, she would bring home a chicken she had stolen. No one molested her, for Aunt Martha paid for the chicken, and as Hope said, perhaps Jett thought it was like having a bill at a store. She had a running account at the neighbor's hen-coops, knowing the bill would be paid.

The children called her a "grave robber." For once one of the neighbors lost a little bird. Their little boy was very fond of it, and was allowed to bury it in the garden. He folded it up in his little pocket-handkerchief, and put it into the hole he had dug, and covered the earth over it. He put up a little wooden paper-knife over the grave, making a nice tombstone, and the design was very appropriate. The top of the knife was carved with a bush, and a bird was sitting on the branches. The point of the knife was down deep in the earth, and he thought everything secure.

Now Jett knew everything going on in the neighborhood. The bird's empty cage had been cleaned, and was standing on a bench outside the kitchen door. Jett had interviewed the cage and tried to get in, but finding the door too small, she had seated herself to think it out, wondering in her mind where the bird had gone. When she heard footsteps, she mounted to her post of observation on the fence; and when she saw the boy bring out the bird and bury it, she was perplexed.

A cat never allows a mystery to go unsolved. After it was all over she waited a suitable time, and then she made an investigation. She walked around the monument, she smelt of it, and she clawed it a little. By the time she had satisfied her curiosity it looked like the Leaning Tower of Pisa. That it moved was probably a suggestion to her, for she began scratching the earth; and it soon fell over, leaving a bit of the grave clothing of the poor little bird exposed. This at once was proof positive, and after scratching away the earth she found the mystery.

Jerking up the handkerchief, she soon landed the little corpse, and then she examined it with a critical eye. No coroner inquiring into the cause of a sudden death could have been more careful. After she had inspected it thoroughly she took one claw in her mouth and started for the house, and never rested till she had with great difficulty deposited that bird in its cage and pushed to the door. Then she went home, satisfied that she had done an act of justice and humanity.

It is needless to say how surprised the family were to find the dead returned to them, and they suspected a mischievous boy who lived near; but when Jett dug up that bird for the second time, there were witnesses, and the deed was brought home to her.

The last burial took place while Jett was shut up. They dared not put up the monument, for they knew she would discover the grave by that. She hunted for a week, but she never found that bird again.

All the neighbors looked upon her as a mysterious element that had come into their midst. They believed in the witches having unlimited power over black cats, and never dared interfere with her; indeed, her good will they were very glad to gain.

Jett was devoted to Hope. She never killed a rat without bringing it with a purr of satisfaction, and was not satisfied till her little mistress had noticed her, and said, "What a good kitty to catch the naughty rats."

There was one place the children called the "cats' paradise." It was down in the corner of Jack's garden. Here catmint grew in rank profusion. The place was neglected, but nature had rioted there, and it was all abloom with wild flowers and weeds.

Here Jett held her afternoon teas and musicales, and she would frolic with her friends in the sweet-smelling grass. Her high soprano would mingle with the contralto and other nondescript parts till they produced a "passion music" so terrible in its results that it required all Jack's strength to separate them.

Why these musicales always ended in a free fight, Hope wondered. Jack suggested that the catmint intoxicated them, for they were usually captured with their mouths and paws full of it, and as much on their fur coats as they could hold. But this state of happiness was not quite as satisfactory to others as it was to the cats and the children.

Jack announced one day that she had been disturbed by the musicales, and the catmint period was drawing to an end. Jack said:—

"She won't outwit me. Aunt Martha will let me plant some over behind your large barn, in that field, and we will dry all we can. Jett shall have her winter supply, and I will treat every cat in the neighborhood."

Jack worked with a will, and before the man Mrs. Thornton had hired to remove and destroy the catmint bed had arrived, it was nearly all transplanted or cut off to dry. They did enjoy that work.

Hope was seated in a wheel chair her father had bought for her, and Jack delighted in wheeling. She superintended all the work.

Aunt Martha allowed the man of all work to plant all that Jack brought him, though she did not think it best for him to take the catmint from Jack's garden.

Jett and Bimbo were very much interested. Bimbo eyed them in solemn silence for a while, then he yelled, "Go ahead! Hurry up! hurry up! She'll get you!" till it did seem as if that clever bird knew everything.

Jett's help was rather doubtful, though her interest was not. She followed Jack back and forth, and at every fresh root he would take up she would turn a somersault in the hole, scratching the earth with all her might; then she would rush back—a picture of yellow earth, black fur, and catmint.

These were happy days, too soon followed by sorrowful ones. As summer waned, and autumn advanced, the first frost cast a blight on the little life so fondly cared for by her friends.

Jack's sorrow, when he was made to realize her danger, was pathetic. He was now constantly with his little playfellow when she was able to see him. It was a picture to see her propped up in bed, Jack sitting by the side, in a little rocker, Joanna in her arms, or if too feeble to hold her, lying by her side, while Jett was curled up at her feet.

Poor, sorrowful Aunt Martha hovered around her darling, ready to attend to her slightest wish. Jett was devoted to her. In this case can be seen what devoted creatures cats and dogs can be if they are made friends of. They seem to realize the approach of that dread messenger, and to be "faithful unto death."

Jett only left the sick child long enough to take a constitutional and her meals. Then she would go back and mew piteously, if the door was closed, to get in to her little mistress. If Hope was asleep, she would jump up on the bed, stand and look at her a little while, perhaps lick her hands, and then lie down where she could watch every movement. If Joanna had fallen on the floor, she would pick her up with her teeth, give her a real shake, as if to say, "What did you fall down for?" and then, jumping up on the bed, deposit her in Hope's arms or by her side.

Never was there a case of greater devotion. She was always pleased to see Jack. She would lick his face and sit in his arms, but on the least movement of her little mistress back she would go and watch her with the deepest affection.

The end came very suddenly. Just at the close of a lovely October day sweet little Hope Farley fell asleep. She had seemed to know that the end was near. She had spoken of her death to her Aunt Martha, saying, "I am so tired, but I do not want to leave you and my dear ones."

She had made her auntie promise that Joanna should be dressed just as they dressed her, and be buried in her arms, saying, "I shall not be so lonesome with my dear dolly, and I know Jack and Jett will come and see me often."

So Joanna had a white cambric embroidered dress just like her little mistress's, that Aunt Martha made (with tears falling on her work), and she was laid in her little mistress's arms. Aunt Martha covered her with flowers, and sheltered her under the sleeve of her little mistress's dress as well as she could, knowing how much would be said about her indulging such a queer fancy of the dear child. As Jack said to her, "I do feel glad Joanna is with her. It seems so hard to put her away alone;" and Aunt Martha agreed with him.

They had the greatest trouble with Jett, to keep her out of the room. Every time the door was open she would hide under the bed. She had taken Joanna twice out to the seat in the garden, where she had so often seen her in Hope's arms, and Aunt Martha had to shut her out doors while she dressed Joanna.

Hope looked lovely, with beautiful flowers around her, and leaves from the plants she had loved. Her father was dazed at her loss, but Aunt Martha and Jack were the real mourners.

How it happened they never knew. They had kept track of Jett all they could, and Jack had petted her, and tried to comfort her, but all to no purpose. She was like a wild cat, crouching down in corners and watching them all. The last night before the funeral Hope was placed in the casket, and it was closed. Jett must have crawled into a corner under the sofa when the door was open, for she was found in the morning, sitting on the head of the casket, as solemn as if she knew she had been watching her dear little mistress.

She was not willing to go to any one, and disappeared till just as the funeral left the house, when she was seen on the opposite side of the street. When they reached the old cemetery, she was noticed behind some shrubs.

Jack got out of the carriage to see if it was Jett, and take her home, but could not find her. They thought it could not be she; but when days passed away and she did not return, they were sure it was Jett who had followed to her little mistress's grave. They sought her everywhere, leaving the outbuildings open, so in case she returned she could get in; but they never found any trace of her again.

There were stories, that they did not give credence to, of a cat's being seen hovering around the grave; but many people did believe that it was Jett guarding the grave of her dear one.

Superstitious people said that she was a ministering spirit sent to guard and comfort the life of that dear little child. That her mission being fulfilled, she went back to those who sent her, perhaps to be still with the dear child in Paradise. Others said she was a witch cat, spared for a little while, to be happy in this beautiful home; but her mission being over, the witches called her back. That perhaps at night she was allowed to visit the grave of the one she had served so devotedly.

But my opinion is, she was just a good, loving cat. She was grateful for all their kindness, and loved little Hope just as all cats love those who are kind to them. She had not been born in that home, as one would know by the strange way she often behaved that she had no training.

Of course her disappearance is hard to account for; but I do believe she could not bear to live in that home after Hope had left it, and she found another one for herself. Of course a cat has a right to an opinion. This is mine.

But does it not show how kind, loving, and faithful cats can be? If properly trained, they make the best companions for children.

Who that ever has seen dear little kittens, so loving and trusting, climbing in the arms of those who are kind to them, can doubt they are given to them for friends?

XXII
WATCH AND CHLOE

MUCH has been said of the benefit of example. Why, then, when a cat follows the example of the people with whom she lives, should she be called "bloodthirsty" if she kills a chicken? She follows her master to the hen-coop, and looks on in wonder when he wrings the neck of one of the chickens he has fed daily. Then when she takes her own method of killing a chicken for her own eating, where is the harm? She could be taught better, of course.

Dogs are taught not to touch game, even when it falls at their feet, till their master gives them permission. Cats would never steal if they knew it was wrong.

Look at my case. After the theft of that meat from the good "philanthropist," I never took anything else. My mistress made me understand wherein it was wrong. I felt very much ashamed, though I could not be blamed. It was one of the most delicious morsels I ever had.

If a cat is not well fed, she will help herself, just as, under the same circumstances, human beings would do the same. It is astonishing how many peculiar traits are brought out when one studies animals.

I heard a story of a cat called Tinker, who lived with a very nice family. They were country people, with a large farm, with horses, cows, dog, and cat, all well cared for, and favorite companions of the children. Nothing was ever killed on that place except rats.

Tinker was a ferocious mouser. She was, however, very fond of all the animals, and the horses would put their heads down to her when she rubbed against their legs. Even the cow did not resent it when she would lick her after she had been milked. They did say that Tinker had been known to help herself to a little, sometimes, before the good Brindle had been milked.

They had hens and chickens in plenty. But they never killed one of their own, always buying their poultry of the farmers around. They were content with selling the eggs in great quantities, for the hens were so well kept that they laid a great many.

Tinker was well fed; and as she had never seen hens and chickens killed, she treated them as if their right to live could not be questioned. She walked out and in the hen-coop whenever she pleased. She had very nice ways, and was never known to go near the pig-pen, that being, in her opinion, not exactly a pleasure ground.

One day the hens were all out in the large field back of the house, when Tinker was walking about on a voyage of discovery. She soon espied three little chickens of a very tender age shivering with cold and sending forth feeble little peeps. She looked around; then mounting on the nest, she sat over them, and they nestled in her warm fur.

Soon a great clacking announced the return of their mother. She was telling all the gossip of the farm to the other hens. She was just as surprised as she could be to see her place filled. She flew at Tinker in great wrath. Tinker just raised her paw and kept her back and sat there as long as she pleased. The mother hen ran about, telling her story to all the coop assembled to see the fun. Even the lordly rooster cocked his comb about, in wise deliberation, over this most unusual occurrence.

The unusual noise drew out the master, who was so well pleased that he called his wife to see Tinker in her position as chicken nurse.

As soon as she saw she was appreciated, Tinker left her post, and there is no doubt the chickens wished their mother had fur on her rather than stiff feathers.

Does not this prove that a cat would be kind to all creatures, were the example before her such as she could follow? Animals learn to kill by seeing man kill everything he is allowed to without drawing upon himself the penalty of the law.

It has often been said that women care more for pets, particularly cats, than men do. I do not think it is true. Men do not make such open demonstrations and decorate their pets in the absurd way that women do, but where they do love them, it is a very lasting affection.

If you follow the course of children who are cruel to animals, you will find they meet with their punishment oftentimes in this world. I have a story to tell in illustration of this fact.

A very charming family lived not very far from Boston, though their home was in quite a country place. The family was composed of a widow with four sons and an only daughter. The eldest son was really the flower of the family. The boys were all full of life, but very unlike their elder brother. Robert was a gentleman and a scholar. Mary, the sister, was his special friend, and he made of her a real chum, telling her all his plans and in every way making a friend of her.

They lived in a grand old house. It had been built by their ancestors some two hundred years. The land about was very beautiful, and they lived in comfortable style, though not really wealthy. They loved the old family horse, and the cow would follow every member of the family. They had a good, big dog; and last but not least a great, dignified cat called Bruno.

The cat was the special pet of Robert and Mary. The younger boys teased him, and he kept out of their way. He well knew how to defend himself, and they were rather afraid of him.

There were no near neighbors. The grounds of their nearest companions met theirs, but nearly half a mile away. As they were not congenial, the distance was rather satisfactory.

Bruno would not notice the poor, wretched, hunted-looking cat belonging to the other place, and she was afraid of every moving thing. The people were very mean, though they kept up a great show of wealth; the servants and the animals about the place were half starved.

Poor Mossy had no one to love her. She had never been petted, and her life was made still more wretched by the loss of her many kittens. At last she disappeared. Then they realized her value, for she was a great mouser, and the place was infested with rats and mice. Knowing their enemy had gone, they returned in full force, and the people tried in every way to find Mossy, but in vain.

After a time the chickens on our friend Robert's place disappeared. They could find no trace of the robber, though they watched very carefully.

Max would bark nights, and Bruno, the cat, seemed to be very uneasy at the same time, as if he heard some intruder. One of the boys would stay out at night till quite late, but the hen-coop was peaceful; and though they tried every means, they never caught the intruder. And the chickens disappeared, all the same.

At last the boys discovered a hole in the back of the hen-coop, where the earth had been dug down and room made large enough for a cat to enter. The boys declared they had seen a cat that looked like Mossy come out of the pine woods at the back of the hen-coop, and they believed she had stolen the chickens.

Robert said, "If it is Mossy, do not harm her, but coax her here and feed her."

Robert had always petted her when he could get the chance, but she seemed to shrink from and distrust every one.

The boys were not of the same mind. They had no love for Mossy, and believed in punishing the one who had stolen the chickens. So they baited a trap with poisoned meat, just outside of the hole, and poor Mossy was caught. She was quite dead; but, not satisfied, they battered her head with stones.

Robert's wrath was terrible when he learned of poor Mossy's fate. He not only cuffed them right and left, but he told them they had forfeited the right to the pleasure trips and fun he had promised them. Robert had a scientific turn of mind, and his experiments were a great wonder and pleasure to the boys, and the loss of his favor was a severe punishment.

The next day, when they went out, they said, "We will take the body of Mossy into the woods and bury it, and perhaps we shall find out where she made her home."

They had laid down the body of Mossy on the grass while they went to dig a grave for her, when a mewing, shrill but feeble, greeted their ears. They looked back, and a most pathetic sight greeted them: the dead body of poor Mossy was completely covered by five little kittens. They were half starved, and were trying to nurse their dead mother. "Oh, ho!" said the boys, "this is what she was up to! She wanted to raise a family all by herself."

The three boys each took a kitten, and, whirling it around, dashed its little life out against a tree, saying, "We will send her orphans after the chicken stealer."

Robert and Mary had followed them, wanting to see that they buried Mossy as they ought to. They arrived on the scene just at the moment when the poor little kittens were killed. Robert rushed forward and with one blow felled one cruel wretch to the ground, while the others fled.

Poor Mary almost fainted at the dreadful sight; but Robert put the two little kittens (that he took from their mother's dead body) into her arms, and as she wrapped them in her shawl, they cuddled up to her so confidingly that it comforted her, for she said, "They shall never know sorrow."

Robert was moved almost to tears. As soon as he could command his voice he said: "God will punish this act of cruelty, this crime. They are my brothers, but I would not lift up my hand to save them from prison."

He then made a grave, and Mary helped as well as she could (with the little kittens in her arms) to put in leaves, and Robert spread out his handkerchief and tenderly laid in poor Mossy and her three kittens. It was a solemn sight. Mary covered them with her handkerchief and a few more leaves, and then Robert filled in the grave.

They carried home the two little orphans in silence. The poor things were very hungry, and Mary fed them and put them into a basket with soft white wool, and as soon as they opened their eyes she was ready with milk and petting, that they might not feel their mother's loss.

Robert was very fond of them. As soon as they could run about he took them up to his den, where all his time was spent in study, and they were perfectly at home. They would dart about, over books, papers, and table, and there was so much electricity about them that Robert named them Castor and Pollux, for he said they were like a flash of lightning in their movements. Of course they were called Cassy and Polly. They were the exclusive property of Robert and Mary, and the boys never dared touch them.

The mother, a confirmed invalid, was never told of the boys' wickedness; for her sister, who had the care of her, with the help of Mary, kept everything of a disturbing nature from her.

Strange as it may appear, their instinct taught the kittens to shun their mother's murderers. They would never go near them; and another very strange thing—they would never, even when hungry, touch a bit of chicken. They never went near the hen-coop, and would run and hide when the hens and chickens were around.

Is there not some psychological explanation of this fact? Did not the spirit of the mother in some mysterious way influence her children?

It was supposed that Mossy, after losing her kittens so often, decided she would take the matter into her own hands and save those she was expecting. She went away, when near the time of their birth, and hid herself in a cave in the rocks, for it was found some time after that she had made a deep cave, digging it out patiently till it was large enough for comfort. Chicken feathers were found spread all around, proving she had thought about the comfort of her children and herself, and provided them a good home. She stole chickens from the neighboring coops, and feasted herself and used their feathers. She certainly displayed human intelligence in her work.

Castor and Pollux grew up to be very fine cats. They were very smart mousers, like their mother, and they were devoted to Robert and Mary. Bruno was quite jealous of them at first; but after a time, finding his importance was not lessened, he gave in, and treated them with politeness. When, one day, Cassy brought a mouse he had killed, and laid it in his arms when he was asleep, he adopted Cassy at once. It was a real picture to see that big, dignified cat with the plump little kittens playing around him. They had no respect or veneration in their intercourse with him. They just loved him as they did everything around them.

Mary would take them in to see her mother sometimes when she had a few hours' relief from pain. The mother would say: "What will you do, Mary, if Robert or you should marry? You cannot both have the kittens, and you surely cannot separate them."

"Oh," she answered, "I shall never marry, and Rob may get a wife who will not love cats, and I shall have them all my own."

When she repeated this to Robert, he said: "I shall never have a home where Castor and Pollux are not welcome. It will be the test I shall apply to the woman, if I ever find one, whom I propose to make my wife, whether she loves cats and is kind to dumb animals."

"You had better not announce the fact; for there are hundreds who would tolerate even a gorilla and pretend to be fond of it for the sake of being the wife of my elegant brother Robert."

He laughed, saying, "Perhaps, in that case, as there are sixty thousand single women to be provided for, it would be better not to advertise."

He was truly in earnest, as was soon proved. The young friend of his sister that he had been very much pleased with, and had paid more attention to than to any other he had met, came to visit Mary soon after this conversation had taken place. She was very pretty and charming, trying to please Robert in every way. Finding he was fond of cats, and hearing with sympathy the story of Mossy, she was very affectionate to Cassy and Polly; but they did not reciprocate, and kept away from her when it was possible.

One day Cassy sat upon her beautiful new hat and crushed the flowers. She flew at him in a great rage, saying: "You horrid old cat! I would not have you around in a house of mine."

She slashed him over with her bag, while he slunk under the sofa in fear and trembling. It was the first abuse he had ever known.

She thought she was alone, and soon left the room with her precious hat. But she had forever ruined her chance of being Robert's wife; for as soon as she left the room he moved the Turkish screen that formed a protection for the window seat where he was lounging with a book, and stooping down he took poor Cassy from under the sofa and carried him up to his den, where he remained with his two pets. They were the only witnesses of the death of his fancy for his sister's friend. When she called Cassy and Polly to her, he well understood why Cassy crept under the table out of her sight.

He became a very successful scientific man, but the brothers met with retribution for their cruel crime. Two of them were victims of a railroad accident, while the third died from blood-poisoning from the bite of a rat he had caught in a trap. Justice was dealt out to them in full.

If young people would test each other's natures by their treatment of animals, there would not be so many deceived and repentant married people.

Castor and Pollux lived to be twenty years old. They seemed to bear a charmed life. They were very fond of each other, but often they would have a pitched battle and retire to separate corners for a while, but it never lasted long. They were soon as good friends as ever.

The lady Robert married was very fond of cats. When she was married, she could not be separated from her pet dog Fido; but she was mistress and soon made them understand they must be friends.

She never allowed either the dog or the two cats to be unjust to each other. It took time and patience, but she persevered, and was successful at last. By judicious treatment she made them the best of friends. It was a very funny sight when Fido would carry some of his candy and put it on Cassy's and Polly's paws, and then bark with delight at his own generosity.

And when her little girl, named Mary, after Robert's sister Mary, who had died just before his marriage, was born, the two cats and the dog were her earliest friends, and they often fought for her favor, each seeming to believe her to be his own special property; but she kissed and cuffed alike, so they were a very happy family.

Cassy and Polly were always to be found in their master's study when he was engaged in absorbing work. They would quietly pore over maps and charts, as full of interest as they would have been had he been their teacher. Their master said he had solved many hard questions while smoothing their soft fur and meeting their intelligent glances. And he could not help saying, "What do you think of it, my friends?"

I think a man like the master of Castor and Pollux a true and grand gentleman. How many might be happy if, like him; they would care for their humble friends. There is no doubt that a cat oftentimes helps out some problem.

My mistress would sometimes take me in her arms and look into my eyes. I could feel that look right into my heart, and I know that I answered it, for she would say, "Oh, Daisy, you have given me an idea." And I would advise my friends, both young men and women, when you have some difficult problem or study, take your faithful friend, the cat, look deep into her eyes while you tell her your perplexity, and see if she does not help you solve the difficulty. There is an electric current that passes into your brain from hers, and clears away the mists from your understanding. Then your kindness to your dumb friend is rewarded by the success you deserve.

There is another story I like very much. It is about a cat and a dog, and they lived in Beverly, in a very beautiful place quite near the shore.

The dog's name was Watch, and the cat was named Chloe. Watch was not a handsome dog, but he was a faithful, good little fellow. He had very short legs (my mistress said, just like a cricket). He was a dark yellow, or what now is called a dull old gold. He had a very broad back, where Chloe could sit comfortably whenever she pleased.

Watch was very humble, and believed in "woman's rights" evidently, for he never offered any resistance when Chloe saw fit to use him for an easy-chair. He would crouch down on his short legs, and solace himself with a good sleep—that was his panacea for every ill. But he never allowed his master, whom he worshipped, to take one step without rising and standing in respectful silence or following him at a distance. This was very exasperating to Chloe, for he would shake her off with scant ceremony to do honor to his master.

But Chloe had no reverence or respect for anything but a good dinner. Many were the cuffs she gave poor Watch, which he bore meekly, because he would rise when his master appeared and disturb her sleep.

He was really a refrigerator color. His fur was short and stiff, his ears were large and prominent, drooping, unless something unusual aroused him. Then his interest only lasted for a moment. He would relapse into the stolid, silent dog they all believed him to be. He identified himself with the family, though he did not join in their sports; but he always knew just what was going on, and would follow them at a distance wherever they would go.

His master was his idol. He seemed to live for him alone. His bright, beadlike black eyes were always fixed on his master's face, and he knew every change of expression. His master would say, "Watch is the only one of my children with black eyes; he takes after me." Years after Watch died there were two little black-eyed girls born, but Watch could not enjoy the sight of them.

Chloe was a calico cat, yellow, with patches of dark and white spots. She was not much prettier than Watch, but the children thought her beautiful and loved her dearly.

Their father had made them a wooden doll, and they were as pleased with it as children of to-day are with the elegant creatures who can open and shut their eyes and squeak out "mamma" and "papa." The children had been brought up to enjoy and believe Bible stories, and they thought the highest honor they could give that doll was to call it by a Bible name. So, after a discussion, they named it Amminadab, for the very reason that it was very hard to pronounce and impossible to understand.

Chloe and Watch were very good friends. To be sure, Watch never dared say his soul was his own in Chloe's presence. Possibly that was the reason they had peace.

Chloe had a very roving disposition. Day after day she would go off into the woods near by, and then Watch would suffer great anxiety. He would go out into the road, and look up and down, and then indulge in a mild bark. He never would go to sleep till she returned, and would meet her with the greatest satisfaction, wagging his short tail and walking around her as if to say, "You have come back, haven't you?" He delighted to see her run up trees, and would look up at her, and bark with pride, never at all jealous of her superiority.

When the children went down to bathe, Watch would attend them as body-guard. They always carried their doll and gave her to Watch to take care of. They would place her on a high rock, while Watch would sit down beside her, with his paws on her dress, to keep her from falling off. They would say, "Watch, take good care of her," and then they were sure he would never leave her. Chloe did not often go with them, for cats do not like the water as dogs do; but she knew where they were and was very impatient for them to return.

One day when their mother said, "Chloe, where are the children?" she ran down toward the water and back again several times.

Their mother laughed, saying, "Go and bring them home." And sure enough, the children were amused to see Chloe on the rock by Watch's side. She took hold of Amminadab by her dress, and tried to pull her away from Watch. But here she was mistaken in thinking he would give her up. He held his ground. He had been told to guard that doll, and guard her he would. Chloe tugged at her dress, tearing it with her teeth, but he held on. Then she fell upon him, and cuffed and clawed him, while he tried to dodge her all he could; but at one hard blow, in defending himself, he loosened his hold a bit on Amminadab, and Chloe, with one good pull, gained the victory and ran home, dragging the poor doll over the ground, bumping her poor wooden head without mercy. This was too much for Watch. He ran in pursuit, but his short legs were no match for her long ones, and she reached home, dropping Amminadab on the threshold long before he arrived.

Then ensued a fight to carry her back, and the master, who always took the part of Watch, had to separate them. He took the bone of contention into the house, and that settled it.

They were sincere friends, however, and later on, when poor Watch was unfortunate, the good heart under Chloe's rough exterior was shown. Watch lost his hearing and then his eyesight, and it was then Chloe came to his aid. She helped him and seemed always to have the care of him on her mind. She hovered around him when carriages drove by, and he, not seeing or hearing them, would sit in their track. She would drag him away by the ear or push him away and share his danger. And he soon followed her slightest touch.

She would often put his food under his nose, for he at last lost even his sense of smell. The sense of feeling he never lost, and would put out his paw, and his poor old heart would beat while he would give forth a cracked and feeble bark when his master touched him—loyal and faithful unto death!

His master could not bear the thought of parting with him, though he knew it must be, for he was in danger of being killed all the time, and, having lost all his senses, he at last refused food, and they were obliged to "put him to rest." Chloe was inconsolable. She wandered about everywhere, searching for him.

One day they saw her lying down on some shining object. They found it was an old collar belonging to Watch that she had found in the attic. She fought when they took it away from her; and when they returned it, she carried it out to the barn and put it in the corner where Watch used to lie.

There were warm sunny places he had selected to rest himself in when he grew tired and sick, and Chloe went to every one of his old haunts and made her bed. She attached herself to the master just as Watch had done, and seemed overjoyed if he noticed her. Very soon the sympathy between them in their mutual loss made them real friends. He would talk to her about Watch, and she seemed to understand all he said. It was a real comfort to him.

It is often said that a dog is more companionable than a cat, and has higher intelligence. That is not true. Cats fully understand everything that a dog does; but a dog is trained, and no one but a real cat lover would ever think of training a cat.

Chloe never regained her bright spirits after the death of Watch. She did not wander off into the woods so often, attaching herself more to the children and her home. She followed the children like a shadow. She could play hide-and-seek in and out the pine trees, jumping out on them in real earnest, and was always the first one to find the hiding place.

On the place was a real old-fashioned well. Chloe was very fond of that well, and the bucket was a real friend. Warm days she would lap the drops of water from its sides, for it was like ice water.

One day a kitten belonging to a neighbor mounted on the side of the well and looked down with wonder into the boundless depth. It was a perilous seat. Chloe, not pleased at the kitten's rashness, ran around the well and in every way tried to call her down from her perch; but she was an obstinate little creature and took no notice of Chloe's evident distress. Finding moral suasion of no avail, quick as a flash she flew up, and, taking her by the nape of the neck, deposited her in safety on the grass, where they had a good romp together; and she never allowed that kitten to go near the well again without her company.

The master would say, "We need not fear for the children; Chloe will never let them approach the well without her company."

It was very funny, one day when the children, returning from a long tramp in the woods, discovered they had left Amminadab behind. There were lamentations loud and long; they were sure they would never again see their dear dolly. Their father asked them if Chloe was with them. Yes, they said, but they did not notice her coming home. Their father walked out into the road, looking in the direction the children had taken. Soon he espied a small cloud of dust and, as it came nearer, a small yellow object, dragging in its mouth something that retarded its progress very much. Soon poor Chloe arrived and laid Amminadab at the feet of her master. She had walked all the way from the pine woods, dragging that heavy wooden doll by the dress, which bore marks of her teeth, having to shut them tight to bear the strain of that weight. She had to take frequent rests, and Amminadab's head was covered with scratches from the stones she had bumped; but she was all there, and when Chloe laid her on the doorstep, she sat down panting and tired, but with the satisfaction of having done her duty just as Watch would have done.

She was petted and praised. Her master brought her out a nice supper of fried fish, and she was perfectly happy. After she had acknowledged all their thanks, she washed her face (cats never pick their teeth in company) and laid herself down on a rug where Watch had enjoyed lying, and slept "the sleep of the just."

She was faithful to the end. To the last day of her life she would never allow Amminadab to be left out of the house without the children, but, taking her in her mouth, would carry her in to her place in the playroom. She would pick up the children's clothes. If they dropped a ribbon or a bit of paper, she would be sure to pick it up and put it on a chair or sofa.

She died peacefully, and her grave was made by the side of her friend Watch.

It is certain that the family never had truer friends than this dog and cat. They all remember them, and count them with those loved ones of whom it is so comforting to say, "Not lost, but gone before."

XXIII
THE STORY OF BLACKIE

ONE of our friends boarded in a family where cats were treated in a cruel manner. Often when my mistress visited her, the tales of woe about poor, ill-used cats made her very sad. Cats always found our friend's room, and proved very loving and grateful for her care. She kept them in her room all she could, always feeding them; and as she had her meals sent to her rooms, she had pieces of meat and always a plenty of milk to give them, and they were very thankful; they loved her dearly. She said they were hunted about, and never knew what it was to have a kind word spoken to them.

One nice cat had several kittens that were kept for the little son of the family to abuse. One of them ran away from him, and was jammed into the crack of a door and killed. Another had its back broken under the rockers of a chair; while the boy had the third one by the tail, swinging it about, banging its head against door-steps, till its feeble moans made the neighbors call to him; and as he paid no heed to them, one good-hearted Irish girl rushed out and, with a good shake, took the kitten in, and ended its sufferings in a pail of water. You do not often see a real, true-hearted Irish girl that is cruel to animals.

The mother of that boy never noticed any complaints made to her of her child's cruelty to animals. She allowed him to do as he pleased with his living playthings, regardless of their suffering.

At last the cat ran away or was stolen, and my mistress's friend said she hoped they would never have another.

A little sister had been born, and at an early age developed the same cruel traits that made her brother a terror to all animals. At last, after some months, they had a black kitten given them. She was about six months old, a beautiful black, and she had very sharp claws. Though the boy was obliged to keep away from her,—for she defended herself with her sharp claws,—her life was wretched. The first lesson she learned was to defend herself, and look upon every one as her enemy.

She had not one friend. No one ever spoke a kind word to her, and she was given wretched food and bones, for the boy devoured every scrap usually given to a cat. Then she was hunted into the cellar to find rats, and her life was one long punishment. No resting place, no nice corner, or bed to call her own—she was an object of pity indeed.

At last a gleam of light dawned on her darkened life. A mouse had been heard in the room of our friend, and Blackie was sent up to catch it. She cowered down in one corner, trembling all over, not knowing what would be done to her. When the lady took her on her lap, smoothed her soft fur, she seemed to realize that there was something besides kicks and blows for her. When laid on a soft wool shawl on the lounge, she testified her delight by "kneading up bread" on the shawl with her claws, till she was tired, then purred out her satisfaction, and at last indulged in a good sleep, though starting and trembling at every sound, for cats are all nerves and sensitive in the highest degree. That night she caught a mouse, and after that was allowed to sleep in the room for a long time, and she effectually cleared the place of them.

When she slept downstairs again our friend had given them a box for her to sleep in, with old blanket pieces folded to make her comfortable. This was to be kept in the passageway just out of the kitchen, that she might keep the rats away.

She had got so attached to her friend by this time that she did not relish being out of her room at all, and early in the morning she would be up at the door, crying like a child to be let in, if the door was closed.

It was a very great trial to this kind-hearted lady, for she could not keep Blackie all the time, and knowing she would be away in summer some months, she was very unhappy about leaving Blackie. She tried to interest the people in the house in her, but it was of no use. The mistress of the house hated Blackie, frequently threatening to get rid of her. She dared not offend her boarder, so she contented herself with abuse of the poor cat on the sly. She did not half feed her, but the cat knew where she could always get food, for the kind friend would buy meat for her and feed her well. Blackie turned from them all. She did not believe in any one but her kind friend, so it was impossible to help her.

All the lady could do when she went away was to speak for her to all of the people she could in the house, and to give the servants money to buy meat and to be kind to her. But she always left with a heavy heart.

At last Blackie was to have her first kittens. She, with that rare instinct that cats have at such times, established herself on the lounge in her friend's room, and if not forcibly removed, would ignore her hunger rather than go down in quest of food. She was determined her kittens should be born in luxury and under the care of her kind friend. Her friend did not fail her. She provided a nice box, all lined and made soft inside; and although she could not have it in her room, she went down every night to see that Blackie was made comfortable.

Poor Blackie! She had a determined will, and escaped from her box the night her kittens were born, and got up to her friend's door, where she cried, and then lay down as near the door as she could, and bore her pains in silence, like the patient creature she was.

As soon as morning came she was carried down and put in her nice box with the seven little kittens she had borne. Her friend took care that they disposed of them humanely, keeping only one. Blackie never rested till she brought up that kitten and laid it in a large chair; then she felt relieved. She would take it up the two flights of stairs, then put it down at her friend's door, while she mewed and scratched till it was opened to her. She was very happy with her dear little kitten, and truly it was a lovely little creature—a real tiger-striped gray.

Blackie was perfectly at home; she cast off the care of her kitten, and rested and got up her strength in this peaceful element. She had avoided the boy tyrant and hid her kitten away from him, and his mother dared not help him find it, fearing Blackie's friend.

The kitten was just the smartest little creature. She soon got big enough to go up to her friend's door, and mew just like her mother, and she cuffed and fought Blackie in a way that proved she would be able to defend herself. Her mother was not so fond of her after she began to show her independence. She tried to keep her in subjection, but found her to be unmanageable. When she went out to parties nights, her mother was very morose over it; and when her first kittens were born, she disowned her altogether. She never would stay in the room with her.

The little kittens were all four allowed to live, and were around the kitchen, under people's feet, abused by the children, and Kitty Gray, as the friend called her, was just wild to get them up into her room. But Blackie, their grandmother, drew the line here. She stood on the stairs, and Kittie Gray with her "No Name Series" (as Miss Milly called the kittens) were never allowed up there.

Poor Kittie Gray! She could not understand it. She had had such a happy childhood, and now the change was fearful. From a bright, happy cat she became a snappish, nervous creature, all the time in fear for her kittens. Sometimes Blackie did try to save the poor little creatures from the children, but it was of no use. Their mother hated her because she had defended herself from that boy, and they kicked and cuffed her till she was obliged to abandon the wretched little creatures to their fate, and the boy and girl tortured them just as they pleased. Their mother said Blackie was a thief, stealing things to eat all the time, and she hated her. She said, as soon as her kittens were born, she would get rid of her.

When the good friend of Blackie heard of it, she talked seriously to the woman. She told her that with her feelings she never ought to keep a cat. She said that Blackie had well paid for her home in keeping them free from rats. She said, "The cat would not steal if you would give her enough to satisfy her hunger." Then she tried superstition as a reason to be kind to her.

"She is a black cat," she said, "and they are supposed to have the power of making or injuring your fortunes. There are people who would never dare turn a black cat from their home, and would consider it a mark of good fortune to have one an inmate of their family. If you get rid of Blackie, you will never prosper. At least," she said, "have it done mercifully."

It did seem as if poor Blackie knew she was doomed. She never was like herself. Though she would go up to her friend's room and cry to be let in, she was very unhappy, and if any friends came in, she would run and hide, instead of remaining to be noticed as she had before. She was the most wretched cat, and all the petting her friend gave her was no comfort to her. She had a premonition of her fate. Kitty Gray dared not go near her, and it was between two fires that their kind friend lived at this time.

She was away for two days, but the servant had promised to look after the cats and earn the money given her for that purpose. On the lady's return at night, as she had company, she had no chance to ask after Blackie. In the morning no little voice greeted her; and later, when she opened her door, Kitty Gray crept in alone. She looked frightened, and began hunting around the room, mewing piteously. She was dazed, poor little creature! by the scene she had witnessed.

The lady said all at once a faintness came over her, and as she fell back on the lounge she seemed to realize what had taken place. She had not believed they would dare do this thing. She rang the bell several times; then the servant came up, looking very much frightened.

"Maggie," said the lady, "where is Blackie?"

The girl hesitated, but at last said, "She is given away."

"That is not true; I want the whole story," said our friend.

Maggie then said she had promised not to speak of Blackie.

"Very well; you can send Miss M. to me, if she is in the house."

Very soon the young lady from the next room came in. She said: "I was just coming in to tell you this sad story. I leave the house next week to go West. Had I not proposed going there, I should not have remained in this house another day. As it is, I have never been downstairs since you left, and I never shall go to that table again."

Then she told her story. She said the night after our friend went away she saw Blackie at her door, and petted her and carried her down to her box and helped the girl give her some food. In the morning she did not get down to the table till late, and then there seemed something very unusual in the atmosphere of the house. She went out as usual to see Blackie, but the mistress of the house shut the door, saying, "That old black cat is dead, and I want to hear nothing about her." The young lady said she was so faint she ran upstairs to her room and burst out crying.

Later, when the servant girl came up, she made her tell the story. She said the girl had been told that if she should let Blackie's friend know how she died, that she should lose her place, but the girl said, "I don't care. I hate her; and as soon as I can I will leave here."

She said Blackie had four kittens. As soon as the last one was born, and poor Blackie lay back exhausted, this fiend in human shape, this cruel woman, took her and thrust her into a tub of water, holding her down with all her strength till her struggles and shrieks ended. It was a wholesale slaughter. Next she put the two good-sized kittens of Kitty Gray in, and then the four helpless ones of Blackie. The boy and girl looked on, dancing and yelling till the cries of the kittens were all still.

The girl said she thought Hell could not be worse than that scene. They were thrown into the city cart, a dreadful sight, and one calculated to harden the hearts of the children, who looked on at the exhibition of these neglected remains.

The lady was speechless. She said she could not bear even to see Kitty Gray, and she wished the poor little creature had been destroyed with the others. She wrote a note, giving a week's notice that her rooms would be at liberty, sent for a carriage, and left the house. She sent a friend to pack her things, and never entered the house again. But she wrote a note to the woman, saying that she knew the laws of the land did not punish such crimes, but she said: "God will avenge that poor black creature; and the sight that you allowed your children to look upon, of wholesale cruelty, will prove a curse to them. You will never prosper."

And she never has. The loss of her two best boarders, then the sickness and death of her husband, the children both of them with some troublesome disease all the time, filled her cup of woe. In one year's time her house was empty, and she was obliged to give it up. Wherever she is, the curse she brought on herself, in the murder of Blackie, will follow her forever; and she will yet see her children made to suffer for the cruel natures she encouraged in them.

Many a murderer can trace back his first wrong act to just such crimes as this one. The first lessons in cruelty are the ones to be dreaded; the children cannot reason, and they follow the example of those older than themselves, and their hearts harden, and no later instructions will ever counteract their influence. And soon the teaching in our institutions supplement their home lessons of cruelty, and they are ready for the pastime of vivisection. No wonder that they are adepts in this criminal abuse of creatures in their power. And God suffers it just as he allows men and women to follow their wicked natures and commit crimes for which they have to pay the penalty. I heard my mistress say this, and I did comprehend it; therefore I do not hesitate to write it even if it does sound too deep for a cat. There are cats—and cats, and I am of the second kind.

I have told you the story of Blackie that you may know what is passing around you all the time. It is heartrending to see the poor cats stealing about, trembling and hiding at the sound of a footstep. Half starved and homeless, what can they do but steal, to satisfy the pangs of hunger? Think how many people steal dress and jewels to decorate their sinful bodies, while cats are satisfied with the forms and clothes their Maker gave them; and they keep themselves clean without the expense of a ticket to the public bath-houses.

There is much said about not giving to the poor, for fear of encouraging laziness. There, again, cats are superior to the human race. You never find a lazy cat. Give a cat a home, enough to eat, and then give her work to do, to clear your house of rats, and she will spend days patiently watching, allowing nothing to divert her attention till she has accomplished her task, and the rats are all killed or driven away.

And they feel well paid by kind words. Cats are invaluable to amuse babies, if you will trust them. I heard a lady say that her baby she left for hours, with the cat sitting on its little crib. She did not like the idea of nurse bottles, as she nursed her baby (that being the fashion at that time); and as baby must have something to go to sleep on, she made of pounded cracker and sugar a pap and put it into little pieces of muslin tied around with a string. It was about as big as a cherry, and the long ends of muslin would prevent the baby from swallowing it. He would go off to sleep contentedly with that comforter in his mouth. Nino had looked on with wide open eyes and even ventured to smell of the little comforters.

One day, hearing the baby cry after a good long hour's sleep, the mother went in, and saw one of the funniest sights. She said the baby was crying, but Nino was lying on her side, with the little comforter in her mouth. From the noise she made and the satisfied expression on her face there is no doubt she enjoyed it, just as one does a new discovery in cooking. When her mistress took it away from her, she made great resistance. After that, when the baby had his comforter, she always laid a fresh one by the side of Nino—a very satisfactory move for her.

She trusted Nino with the children, and Pussy seemed to find as much pleasure in playing with them as she would have found with cats. There was never any nice thing given to the children of which Nino was not given her portion. They never enjoyed their own unless Nino had her full share.

Cats are invaluable in stores. There is no doubt they often prevent robberies and protect their master's property. In a grocery store they do good service. They keep away rats and save a great deal from destruction.

A nice grocer told my mistress that he would not take any sum of money for his cat. He had a very large gray cat, and he might always be seen walking about as if master of the store. His bright ribbon bow on his neck made him doubly attractive to all the children around. He walked over the boxes and cases, with velvet paws, and never was known to break or destroy anything. He would lie quite happy in the window where the sun came on him and would sleep for hours. But let any one presume on his not hearing, and he would find a very wide-awake cat.

Dick never allowed cats to visit at the store. He would drive them out with tooth and nail. But he evidently visited his own friends, for some days he would be away for hours, though he never was absent nights, his master seeing that Dick was in his box, on his rug, before he closed the store.

The grocer's daughter was very fond of cats, and Dick was a prime favorite. One evening, on returning home, she found a little kitten on the doorstep. It was not more than two days old. It appealed to her heart at once, and she decided to keep it. She gave it some milk in a saucer, but it did not know how to lap it, and she gave it a few drops on her finger. From the way it drew her finger into its mouth she got an idea. She had seen dolls' nurse bottles, and she bought one, filled it with milk just warm, and the little kitten took to it at once. It was so happy, sleeping peacefully with that bottle in its mouth, that every one who saw it was delighted. One friend suggested that the girl should exhibit the kitten in the window of her father's store.

It was a dear little black and white kitten, and lying in a basket lined with blue, a blue ribbon on its neck, and the nurse bottle in its mouth, it was a lovely sight. A place was made in the large window, a big box put in, and the basket put on it, and then the crowd were treated to this little show. Not only children, but men and women, crowded the sidewalk; and the exclamations of delight and admiration proved how deep a hold cats have on real true hearts. The grocer facetiously reminded them that as they had all enjoyed this free show, they might now come in and patronize him, saying milk was expensive, and nurse bottles consumed a great deal of the best; that now he had an extra mouth to feed, he must get more custom. His joke was appreciated, and in a very few days he found that the increase of trade, due to the charming picture in his window, was really worth the experiment. And after the people had once bought of him, his kind heart and the very nice quality of his goods made them friends and customers from that time.

But Dick! Wasn't he as mad as a March hare. He looked upon the nurse bottle as an infernal machine, and the little orphan as a fraud. He would not go near the basket, but took a seat where he could measure every drop of milk that was consumed; and although he had always scorned milk as too weak for him, he would hang around the milk-can, and once, when it was not given to him, he threw over the can, spilling all the milk, and then walked away, as if to say, "Now I hope you will give me my share." And they never after that overlooked him, for he developed quite a love for what he had before despised.

His master said he had every reason to be grateful to cats as well as fond of them, for they cleared his store of rats; and one large yellow cat he had when he first kept a store, had saved him from being robbed. The thief had got in through a window, and had made some excellent selections from the boxes and cases, when the cat, seated on a high shelf, knocked over a tin cracker box, and that fell against another, and down went the whole shelf of tins, with a noise like thunder. The man fled, leaving his tools behind him, probably thinking the store was filled with armed men. Pretty good work for one cat!

It seems to me the best combination a safe could have would be a dog and a cat. At the least provocation they would fight, and this would intimidate intruders.

XXIV
RETRIBUTION

A GREAT deal has been said about chloroforming animals. I should prefer this mode of leaving the world to any other. Miss Eleanor was so unhappy over hanging, that the desire to have criminals disposed of in that way was one of her often expressed wishes. If it must be that one murder should follow another,—"a life for a life,"—why should it be a cruel one? Justice would be satisfied.

Miss Milly said, "Oh, that would not be satisfactory to those who delight in punishing their fellow-creatures."

While the law will allow such exhibitions, reserved seats, and tickets to witness the taking of life, and all the etiquette of a first-class bull fight in Spain, just so long will they persevere in the most barbarous way of taking life. It is murder just the same, however it is done.

Sometimes we really see retribution follow crime. There is no doubt it is always punished, though it is not given to us to know how it is done. In the story I am about to relate we can plainly see just how swiftly retribution followed the sin.

A friend told my mistress the tale, and it made my hair stand on end. I suffered so deeply in thinking about it that I know I can tell it in a forcible manner. Tales of this kind, however we may dislike to hear them, must be put in black and white before we can reach the hearts of those in whose power rests the future of that crime called vivisection.

Millions of innocent victims are offered up every year in the name of science. It is simply pandering to the low animal craving for cruelty. No man or woman can witness the torturing of helpless creatures and come out of the ordeal innocent. Why is the cannibal worse than the doctor who uses his knife on helpless creatures, teaching a class of young people to do likewise? Is life safe when the fiendish craving to operate comes upon him? Would his wife or his child be sacred? Would he not practise on them?

And now, as this all-absorbing subject has driven me all around "Robin Hood's barn," I will tell my story. An elderly lady who was very fond of cats told the story to her daughter, and from her it came to my mistress. A niece of this lady, a beautiful girl, had married a young doctor. Her friends were not pleased with the match, but could not influence her. She was young, beautiful, and rich. She was her own mistress, being an orphan, and under no obligation to obey her aunt unless she would do so willingly. It is a very true saying that love is blind. She could see no flaw in her idol.

For two years she travelled in Europe with her aunt, the separation being a great trial to the lovers. On her return they were married, and his devotion made her life perfect. When their first child was expected, they felt that nothing would be wanting to complete their happiness.

One year from the date of their marriage she died, and a few hours after her beautiful little son followed her. Her husband was prostrated with grief, and in two months from the day of her death he left his home and sought in travel to forget his sorrow. Three years after, he died in Rome, of fever.

His friends believed he had recklessly thrown away his life. Without his wife he cared not to live. But there was a mystery that many friends suspected, but the truth was never made public. The aunt held the key to the mystery and revealed the sorrowful secret to her daughter.

Alice was one of the most sensitive girls. She never would tolerate a falsehood. She had one master passion, and that was love of animals. Her horse knew her voice and would follow her about like a dog. But of all her pets, she loved cats the best.

Some time before her engagement to Dr. G. she had a beautiful little kitten. She seemed to live for that little creature. It was always in her arms and seemed to know as much as a child. When it was eight months old it disappeared under the most mysterious circumstances. Search was made, and great rewards were offered, but all of no avail. She mourned for it, and had it been a child she could not have suffered more.

She fell ill of low fever, and her friends were very anxious about her. They never mentioned Little Blossom to her, and she never had another cat. After her engagement and marriage she was very happy, but never could speak to her husband about her loss, and he knew nothing of her love for Little Blossom. They were seldom separated, but two months before her death her husband left her to visit a patient in a neighboring town.

As she was well and cheerful, he did not feel any hesitation at leaving her, though he expected to be away all day. He was surprised, on his return, that his wife was not watching for him as usual. He ran up to their room and, finding the door locked, called to his wife to open the door. Receiving no answer, he was alarmed and, going through his dressing-room, entered the room. The odor of chloroform caused his heart to stand still with fear. His wife lay on the lounge insensible.

He threw open the windows and used every means in his power to restore her, and she at last revived. With a look of horror she recoiled from him, releasing herself from his arms in frantic haste. He thought she had lost her reason, and when she again became unconscious he took her in his arms and carried her into her room, where he laid her on the couch, and she soon revived. Very tenderly he soothed her, asking her why she had used a dangerous thing like chloroform so recklessly. He remembered that she had, before her marriage, used it for neuralgia, but since he had the care of her he had never allowed it.

She looked with a dazed expression. She trembled all over if he touched her, and made no answer to his words of tenderness. He telegraphed for one of the best physicians and a nurse. And then, with the aid of her maid, who was very much attached to her mistress, he made her as comfortable as possible.

The maid could give no explanation of the cause of her sickness. Her mistress had received several letters, and had been shut up in her room writing for some hours. She had taken her some toast and tea, though she did not care to take it. She thought she had taken a chill, for she was shivering and looked very white. She said she would sleep, and did not wish to be disturbed. So the maid left her, and had heard nothing of her since, till called by him on his return.

Though conscious when the doctor and nurse came, she closed her eyes and never spoke a word. After an examination the doctor said, "She has evidently received some shock that has unbalanced her mind." He advised her husband to keep away from her, as the moment he came near her she trembled and shrunk away from him.

It was torture to her husband, but his knowledge taught him that the doctor was right—that the nearest and dearest are always turned from by the diseased mind. Though he never left the dressing room, he kept out of her sight.

Two days from the time she was taken sick she died, and her little son followed her a few hours after. She never spoke to them, though they believed her to be conscious. Their agony and grief did not move her at all, and in the last few hours convulsions prevented any attempt to make her speak.

This was a crushing blow to her husband. To lose her without one word prostrated him. He was to know a deeper sorrow—one that would admit of no consolation. It was a long time before he could look over her papers; but at last it was necessary, and he aroused himself. Then came retribution indeed.

A package met his eye, on opening her desk, directed to him in the handwriting of his wife. The date on the outside convinced him that she had written it soon after he had left her that fatal morning. It contained a letter in a masculine hand, but the letter from his wife he read first.

From that moment his life was ended. He spoke to no one of his friends of his sorrow, giving the charge of their home into the hands of the aunt with whom his wife had lived, and then he left his home, to travel alone.

The letter from his wife, and the one she had received that had caused all her sorrow, was sent to her aunt, at his death, with a letter he had also written. The letter from his wife explained all. She wrote him that after reading the enclosed letter all love for him had died out of her heart, leaving only disgust. She could not endure the thought of him as her husband. She was determined rather than live with him she would take her own life and her child's. She could read only cruel thoughts in his face, and her life would be filled with the dread that she and her child would be subjects for his knife.

"My dear Little Blossom was like a child, and I can see her delicate limbs quivering while you tortured her. I should go mad to live with you, for her dear little face would always be before me."

She had evidently fought with her weakness, to finish her letter, for the writing was almost unintelligible.

He at once recognized the handwriting of the other letter, and he knew that there was no appeal from the truth. He could only say in anguish of heart, "It is just." The letter was directed to her, in her maiden name, and had been forwarded to her by her aunt. By some mistake it was over a year since it had been written, and with other papers was found by her aunt when she opened her house after a long absence.

It was from one of her old friends, a gentleman of high standing, holding a very important position in a neighboring city. The news of her marriage had never reached him, else the letter would never have been written. He had known her from childhood and had loved her hopelessly. His letter stated the fact that a power stronger than his own will obliged him to write to her, and save her from marriage with a man who would surely make her unhappy.

"If I cause you great sorrow, in this terrible relation, it may save you from a life-long unhappiness. Doctor L., my cousin, whom you well know, is my authority, and will swear to the truth of my story. Willard C., your little friend and neighbor, will also vouch for its accuracy, for he took an active part in the scene of which I write.

"Dr. L., as you well know, is a classmate of the man to whom you are engaged. And as he was a frequent visitor at your home, and a great friend of your aunt, you will know there is no appeal against his report. He returned from Germany last week, and when he asked my sister regarding news of his old friends, she spoke of your engagement.

"'Impossible,' he exclaimed, 'of all things this is the most unaccountable.'

"'Why?' said my sister; 'they are very fond of each other, and you are not so shabby, because you have broken with him, to grudge him his happiness, for he is devoted to her. You will admit it is a good match.'

"'Yes,' he said, 'so it looks to the world, but he never ought to marry her.'

"Then he changed the subject, though my sister tried to get at his reason for speaking in this manner. After she left us, I at once insisted on an explanation. Then to my horror and disgust I heard this fearful story.

"My cousin said: 'You know my love of animals and my opposition to vivisection. I have never allowed myself to listen to or assist in any act of this nature. You know my intimacy with Dr. G., and I never for one moment suspected him of the cruelty of which I proved him guilty.

"'Visiting Alice M. so often, I knew all her feelings in regard to animals, and I knew that her love for cats was the master passion of her life. Her last pet was a beautiful little kitten. You surely remember it? She called it Little Blossom.

"'One evening I called on her and learned from the servant that Miss Alice had been ill for some days.

"'On my way home I had to pass Dr. G.'s office, and as I had some business with him, I thought I would call. I found him very busy. Two young students were waiting to accompany him to the classroom. He invited me to go with them, saying, "We have a most interesting subject to-night." I never thought to ask the nature of the study, and finding an old friend in the outer room, I remained talking with him.

"'Soon cries the most agonizing came from the next room, and my friend, an old physician said: "This is hellish work! G. is a fiend when he is at it. I must go and prevent all the cruelty I can."

"'Some power stronger than my own will made me follow him. Dr. G. was the actor in one of the cruellest cases of vivisection. A lovely little kitten about eight months old, a pet kitten evidently, he was torturing, without the least pretence of anæsthetic. Its cries were fearful, but there was no release for it. I cried to him to give it something to deaden the pain, but he was deaf to my request. If ever a man's face was transformed to that of a demon, it was that man's.

"'Two of the students, to their credit be it said, turned away sick and faint, while one of them, Willard C. cried out, "My God! it is Alice M.'s pet, Little Blossom."

"'I gave one spring forward, and—yes, it indeed was dear Little Blossom, her lovely eyes starting from her head, her soft fur matted with blood, while her intestines were exposed to his cruel hand, to be tortured. I tore a long scarf from my neck, and finding a bottle of chloroform near, I saturated it with it and covered the dear little kitten, holding it down with my breast till every sound was still. It was a fearful task, for I was almost overpowered by the chloroform, and Dr. G. fell upon me like a madman despoiled of his prey. But others came to my aid, and Willard C. took the body of the little victim, saying he would bury it himself.

"'To Dr. G. I said: "I will never take your hand again in friendship. Professional honor requires silence, and in this case sympathy with the owner or the victim will allow you to escape punishment. You know there is a law against taking a pet animal."

"'He was in a great rage, saying, "That is not your business. I bought her of a boy, supposing she was his property. I do not think you are much of a doctor if you shrink from procuring the knowledge so necessary to science, however painful the ordeal."

"'"Never would I be a doctor," I answered, "if I must also be a fiend. Heaven grant you may never have wife or child, for they would not be safe from you, if you needed subjects."

"'He laughed a scornful laugh, saying, "My wife, if I ever have one, will be obliged to you."

"'And now, great Heaven! he is engaged to the loveliest and dearest woman I ever knew, and she is the mistress of Little Blossom whom he murdered.'

"'It must be prevented,' I said, as soon as I could control my feeling, for the fearful tale my cousin had so feelingly related, made me sick. 'She shall never be his wife. I will prevent it, even though I have to tell her this heartrending story. If she should discover the truth after her marriage, it would kill her.'

"I could not sleep that night. I could see Little Blossom in your arms, with her blue bow on her neck, just under one ear, and I could feel her soft little paws, when she would give them to me when you told her to. I could hear you say: 'Jack, I love her better than I could love a child. If anything should happen to her, it would kill me, for I mean to keep her all my life.'

"And then the face of that man, as he bent over that innocent little creature! Even when she tried to lick his hand it did not touch his heart.

"Can you blame me for telling you this? I know you so well that I do not fear that the loss of such a fiend will ever trouble you. I know your love will die at once, and Little Blossom will be avenged. And I cannot answer to my conscience if I allow you to marry this man. Wife or child would not be safe with a man who has entered into this compact with Satan, called vivisection. Let no mother ever trust her boy after he has willingly assisted in this cruel pastime.

"Show him this letter, if you wish, and Willard C. will tell you where he made the grave of your dear little pet."

After Dr. G. read that letter he no longer needed a clew to the loss of wife and child. Little Blossom was avenged. But at what a fearful cost!

There are often advertisements seen in the daily papers and great rewards offered for lost pets,—dogs and cats. Never expect to find them. The doctors will pay more than the offered reward for nice, well-cared-for dogs and cats; and boys have no regard for those who feel the loss of their pets. It is to get the highest price.

Is it not the duty of every one who can have influence to use it in behalf of the dumb creatures who appeal to their mercy? They cannot speak for themselves.

XXV

EVENTIDE

WE are still in our pleasant rooms, and life is very quiet and happy. Each day I grow less able to go about. I have no inclination to leave our nice room. It is really true I am growing old. I can hear only in one ear; but, oh my, don't I hear quickly in the other! The sense of smell has grown stronger. I think I could smell a rat one mile away. My eyesight is good. I do not believe even a Boston-born cat ever wears glasses. Their literary tendencies do not need to be advertised by glasses.

But alas! there are other indications of old age. I love to lie quiet, looking in the fire, where I see pictures of the past. My appetite is good, but I am very particular about my food, and if it does not please me, I am irritable. Unless the boys or some friends I love come in, I do not feel inclined to make myself agreeable. It is a real pleasure when Will takes me on his knee, and I can stick my claws in, just as I used to, scratching gently, while he says, "Oh, Daisy, you are at your old tricks!"

But it makes me sad after they have gone. I look in the fire and see the dear little boys of long ago, dressed so cunning and always so full of fun. To know that they are no longer mine! These smart young men have taken their places. Then, indeed, I feel I am an old cat and nearing the end. I have learned now the meaning of "the beginning of the end." I realize that I must finish my book at once, before I get too old to write at all. My thumb is rather stiff and rheumatic, and my "index claw" not quite as sharp a pen as it used to be, but I think I shall be able to finish my work.

There is one thing very true. No one realizes my great age. Friends come in daily, and say, "Oh, Daisy, how lovely you are! and your tail is just perfect." Of course I know it is true. My tail is just lovely, and my fur is as soft and luxuriant as it was years ago. But when they say, "She is beautiful," that arouses all the "old cat Adam" in me, for I suppose that is the part of us that dies last. After having all my life behaved like a gentleman, with all his virtues, and none of his vices, now, in my old age, to be called "She" is more than I can bear. The advanced woman cat may, like her superiors, have a desire to be men; but no gentleman cat would ever care to change his nature or sex. Just because my name is Daisy, they seem to think I am a "Miss Nancy," and adapt their conversation to suit an inferior intellect.

One young girl came to visit us one day, and we were tired enough of her. She had no brains and soon used up all her small talk. Then she gushed over me. It made me sick. I opened my eyes wide at her. This pleased her so much that she nodded just like a donkey, and clucked at me just as if she thought me a hen. Then she repeated that awful silly thing with no sense in at all:—

"'Pussy Cat, Pussy Cat, where have you been?''I've been to London to see the Queen.'"

Her voice was thin and pitched high, and it made me tired and cross. She looked for approval and got disappointed. I backed away from her and swelled up my tail till it was as big as a muff. She was rather frightened, but my two friends laughed. They understood that I was insulted by such childish nonsense. As if I had a mind no deeper than that silly stuff!

I wanted her to know that "Washington" and the "President of the United States" and his wife would be much more attractive to me.

London and the Queen! There are snobs enough to visit them without a cat joining the crowd. I have no doubt the Queen is a nice old lady, but then there are so many nicer ones who earn their own living that I can see every day. Such a journey would be useless. I have never heard she was fond of cats. If she had been, they might be treated better by those who follow after and pin their faith on royalty.

I did get very nervous over that silly "Pussy Cat." It ran in my head, and my nice fire pictures were filled with the maudlin trash. And I was heartily glad when Miss Eleanor said, "Now we will have a little of Dickens to clear the atmosphere." That calmed my nerves, and I fell asleep, and I also fell off of the hassock, where I had perched myself.

The other day I heard Miss Milly say that she scarcely ever took up a paper without finding some interesting anecdote of a dog or cat. Miss Eleanor said, "What interesting stories we could tell of the pets we have known!"

I just laughed to myself, thinking how surprised they would be when they found my manuscript containing many of their nice stories. I never forget stories I hear, and I hear many I would like to repeat if I had space. Here is one, however, I cannot overlook.

A friend of ours had a beautiful maltese cat named Primrose. Primrose had four kittens. They were just perfect, and she was very proud of them. The mistress decided to keep them all, for the children were delighted with them. As they were living that summer in a large old farmhouse, they had plenty of room. Primrose had a large clothes-basket for her nursery, with a nice rug inside. A more luxurious place could not have been found for a home. Indeed, had she been a society cat, feeling the necessity of giving importance to her home, she would, like "human society people," have called her home "Catmore," "The Mewes," or "Pussy Villa." But she was content to call it what it really was,—a good homelike clothes-basket, with beauty and goodness enough inside to allow of its being nameless.

One day one of the children tied a red ribbon around the neck of Primrose. She looked so charming that the other children gave up their pretty hair ribbons to decorate the kittens. There were pink, blue, and yellow. The fourth one was red, like the mother's. It was a beautiful sight. The basket looked like one huge bouquet.

Primrose was away when they were decorated, and on her return she looked with surprise at the brilliant objects in her home. She gave one "cat call" of surprise. This aroused the kittens, and they climbed up the side of the basket and mewed for their dinner. Primrose looked at each one, as if to make sure they were her kittens. Then she jumped into the basket, boxed all their ears, and tore off every ribbon, with the exception of the red one like her own. This was her way of saying; "Stick to your mother's color; it is red. I will not allow children of mine to indulge in such foolish masquerading!" She only made them naughty little kittens, for they did crowd their little sister, with the red ribbon, almost out of the basket. They whispered and licked and played with each other, but would not speak to her.

The next day, however, the children, finding that Primrose preferred her own taste in ribbons to theirs, brought red ribbons for them all. Then the mother was satisfied. Was not that a proof that Primrose could tell one color from another?

I have one great pleasure—I can go out every fair day. I climb on the fence, but do not go away from our garden: for in the next house is a dog, and he is a poor, evil-dispositioned creature. He seems to hate me. Why he should want to make me answerable for his unhappiness, I cannot understand. Just as soon as I appear on the fence, he barks and barks till all the neighborhood is disturbed. I do not notice him, for I know it is a free country, and I have as good a right to the fence as he has to his garden.

Norah, the girl where we live, is very kind to me. She keeps the window open, and I can jump in just when I please. The good kind old "gentleman of the house" speaks very kindly to me, and I know he understands me, for one day when I reached over when that dog was barking, and hissed right in his face once or twice just to aggravate him, this nice old gentleman laughed, and said, "Smart Daisy!" And I enjoyed it. When I got over my madness at night, all alone in my basket, all asleep around me, I did think how sad it was, when I ought to be at peace with all the world, knowing that my life would soon end, to go and irritate that poor dog by hissing at him; it made me feel ashamed. But then, I suppose I shall do it again unless I stay in when he barks.

There was a very nice cat belonging to some people who had recently moved into one of the houses near. He was a real "out and outer." I never heard such a voice or such sentiments before. He said he wanted to kill! It was his mission! Let the rats and mice in the neighborhood beware! He was there. That was enough; they were doomed. He would make that back yard a battle-field.

I was carried right off my feet by his eloquence. "Good heavens!" I thought, "is his name 'Gladstone' or 'Bismarck'? What a loss to me! I shall never find another rat; he will kill them all."

When weeks and weeks passed on, and I had killed a few, though I did not tell him, he blustered so, I thought he had killed dozens. The nice cat in the next house told me that he had never killed one. She said, "He is a real coward." He is just like some men—all talk and brag, "great cry and little wool."

I did like that cat. She said she was very soon going into the country to live. She preferred it to the city. She said where she had lived there were six cats. She liked them, but preferred a change. They were all old cats and did not care to play. Three of them had no teeth, and all the soft pieces of meat were given to them. But they were very poor company. She could not help them, and was glad of a change; it was too much like "The Old Ladies' Home" for her. One of them, she said, was so crazy after valerian that it was given to her all the time, and it made her just ugly and very quarrelsome.

"Well," I remarked, "I am very glad to know of cats that are cared for. There are enough suffering around us to make our hearts ache."

"Yes," she said, "and I could tell you tales that would chill your blood."

I begged her not to. I told her I had seen enough to make me very unhappy, as I could not help them; but she would tell me one.

She said: "On this very street I saw a nicely dressed young man chase a poor cat, a half-starved creature, into a sewer hole and beat her in with his cane; then some boys joined him, and the boys filled in the opening and stayed there shouting and yelling till she must have been suffocated. And this fiend in shape of man came away, laughing. If we could read the papers and knew his name," she added, "probably we should read he had battered his wife's head with a shovel or killed his old father."

I went home with a heavy heart. I had not felt well for some time, and I could not bear to live in such a wicked world. I did not look out of the window very often, for fear I should see that sewer hole and the ghost of that poor cat peeping out.

I cannot help them. All I can think of to comfort me is that I am with people who have all their lives done all they could to help and protect the poor and afflicted, and every animal they could do for has been made happy. And I rest in peace, for I believe that a higher power has guided me, a poor cat, to write this little book, that my life and the many tales of woe I have listened to and here repeat may go forth and do their mission.

I feel that the end is near, and I know that the loving care I have had through my happy life will be mine, for I know we shall meet again. I shall watch for my loved ones at the gate of Paradise.

It is eventide. The glowing tints have faded from my life picture, but the beautiful twilight remains. And when I have crossed to the "golden shore," I hope my memory will come back to my loved ones like the beautiful afterglow of a perfect sunset.

To all the dear friends who have known and loved Daisy I would say an affectionate good-by till we meet again.

THE END

Made in the USA
Las Vegas, NV
19 April 2025

21106039R00066